THE GAMBLER

THE GAMBLER

by

FYODOR DOSTOEVSKY

TRANSLATED AND
WITH AN INTRODUCTION BY
ANDREW R. MACANDREW

W · W · NORTON & COMPANY

New York · London

First published as a Norton paperback 1981

Library of Congress Cataloging in Publication Data

Dostoyevsky, Fyodor, 1821–1881.
   The gambler.

   Translation of: Igrok.
   I. MacAndrew, Andrew R., 1911–   II. Title.
PG3326.I4   1981   891.73′3   81–1494

ISBN 0-393-00044-3   AACR2

W. W. Norton & Company, Inc. 500 Fifth Avenue,
New York, N.Y. 10110
W. W. Norton & Company Ltd. 25 New Street Square,
London EC4A 3NT

2 3 4 5 6 7 8 9 0

INTRODUCTION

A GAMBLER'S GAMBLER

Dostoevsky was a man swayed by passions. Two of these, his lamentable love for Apollinaria Suslova and his obsession for gambling, overlapped.

He met Suslova in 1860, and their unhappy romance was an on-and-off affair until it petered out in 1866. His tragic involvement with gambling began in 1863 when he was on his way to Paris to join Suslova. He stopped off at Wiesbaden to have a go at roulette, hoping to put right his disastrous financial situation. That was the beginning. His gambling passion was to hold him until 1871, when, after a last disaster, he gave it up in disgust.

The object of his other passion, Suslova, was a statuesque, somewhat coarse-featured beauty whom literary critic Rozanov—later her husband—described thus:

> She resembled Catherine de Medici. She could have lightheartedly committed a crime. She could have killed. She was one who would have enjoyed firing from her window at the Huguenots on St. Bartholemew's Eve. I know people who were completely conquered and dominated by her.

Actually, she was one of those women who go in for self-improvement, attend all sorts of lectures, voice all sorts of opinions, political and otherwise, but are actually mostly preoccupied with the picture they present to themselves and the world at large. Even back in St. Vladimir's high school, she seems to have struck her principal as rather independent. In his official report, he says:

> Suslova is a person who cannot be trusted. She wears dark glasses and has her hair cut short. Furthermore, she seems very independent in her judgments and does not attend church services.

The beautiful young Suslova hoped that the famous, middle-aged Dostoevsky would help her "to find herself" and to realize the potentialities that she felt in herself. She wrote to him asking him to arrange a meeting. They met. Soon afterward, she gave him a short story she had written, which Dostoevsky published in *Vremya (Time)*, the magazine he was running.

Judging from Suslova's own diary, the love affair did not have the results she had expected. In no time she loathed her middle-aged lover, who instead of offering her strong moral and intellectual support, proved to be weak and vulnerable. And, indeed, he himself was looking for youth and vigor in her, for something that could make him forget his financial worries and his sick and nagging wife. Nevertheless, she became addicted to him in a way—he became, as she puts it in her diary, her "indispensable enemy." And so, when Dostoevsky decided to go abroad to escape his creditors and his family, Apollinaria Suslova declared that she could not help but come with him.

They decided to leave in the late spring of 1863. But the liquidation of the magazine *Vremya* took more time than had been expected and Dostoevsky had to delay his departure. Suslova, however, wouldn't wait. She packed and left for Paris by herself. He was to join her when he was through with his business.

Dostoevsky set out late in August, but before he met Apollinaria again, he met roulette.

He left the train in Wiesbaden and went directly from the station to the casino. To a man who had been hounded by money problems all his life, the idea that all those problems could be solved within one hour at the gambling

2

table was really fascinating. He wanted to see. He saw and was nauseated, shocked and enthralled. He risked a small sum, won, risked again, won again and went on winning, finally winding up 10,400 francs ahead—and it must be remembered that an 1863 French franc had considerably greater purchasing power than a 1980 U.S. dollar. Dostoevsky was elated. He rushed out of the casino and was about to board the train for Paris when it suddenly occurred to him that he had a good chance of turning the ten thousand francs into a hundred thousand. He returned to the casino. At the end of the day he had lost half but still carried off the respectable winnings of five thousand francs.

He was very pleased with himself. He wrote about his exploit to his sister-in-law in Russia. Amusingly enough, however, he asked her to keep it a secret from his stepson, who "is still naive enough to imagine that one's life could easily be founded on gambling."

In Paris a terrible blow awaited him: Suslova informed him that he was too late. She had fallen in love with a handsome Spaniard called Salvador. She was through with Dostoevsky.

But soon it was apparent that, for the Spaniard, Suslova was only one in a long series of women, and that he was already busy with the next. She could only try to forget that fickle man. Dostoevsky suggested then that they travel together, like "brother and sister," to take her mind off her unhappy love.

During the trip she, at least, felt very much like a sister toward him—oh, a very irritable, impatient sister, but certainly not in the least incestuous. To him, however, her vigorous physical presence, so close at hand and so hopelessly out of reach, was a constant torture. And often, completely exasperated and humbled by Suslova in the hotel, he would rush out to the casino, if the town they were in happened to have one, and gamble throughout the night, winning, losing, raising some cash on Suslova's jewels, losing again, writing to friends for help. . . .

Finally, for several reasons, Dostoevsky had to go back to Russia. His wife's health had taken a turn for the worse, he was getting tired of the suffering inflicted on him by Suslova, and he had begun to despair of ever redeeming his financial situation through gambling. Besides, he felt a great urge to be back in Russia and to write.

They parted in Turin. She went to Paris and he started on his way home. However, he stopped over at Homburg, where he lost every penny he had with him. He wrote to Suslova for help. She pawned her gold watch, borrowed some money from her friends, and sent it to her former lover.

When at last Dostoevsky reached Moscow, things there were hardly such as to make it easy for him to sit down and write a novel. His wife was dying, and he himself had to rush off to Petersburg to work with his brother Michael on putting out a new magazine, *Epokha (The Epoch)*, to take the place of the defunct *Vremya*. So he spent the next months commuting crazily between Moscow and Petersburg, between his wife's sick bed and his brother's ill-starred enterprise. Then, within four months, he lost both his wife and his brother (in April and July, 1864).

Back in 1863, while traveling with Suslova and losing money at the spas they stayed in, Dostoevsky had conceived the idea of a novel centered around the roulette table. His early idea about the book can be gauged from the following letter he wrote to his friend Strakhov from Rome on September 18, 1863:

> For the time being I have nothing ready, but I have what seems to me rather a good plan for a story. . . . The main character will be a Russian living abroad. You know the type—last year, our magazine devoted quite a bit of attention to these Russian expatriates. . . . I'll try to portray a straightforward man who, while quite acceptably educated and sophisticated, is yet a very incomplete human being. He has lost all faith and yet he does not dare to be an atheist; he rebels against all

4

authority and yet fears it. It makes him feel better to think that there is nothing for him to do in Russia and that is why he ruthlessly condemns all those who appeal to expatriates to return to live in Russia.

I can see that central character as if he were standing alive before me. And I am sure that, when my story is finished, it will be worth reading. The main point is that all his vital sap, all his energies, his impetuosity and boldness will be absorbed by roulette. He is a gambler, but not just an ordinary gambler, just as Pushkin's Stingy Knight is not just an ordinary skinflint. . . . My hero is, in his way, a poet, but he is ashamed of the way his poetic feelings are expressed and he feels its ugliness deeply. Nevertheless, his need to risk something ennobles him in his own eyes. The story will cover three years, during which he plays roulette.

Now, since *The House of the Dead* has attracted the public's attention as a portrayal of convicts in a way that no one who had not seen them with his own eyes had described them, this story will also attract attention, being a very detailed description of roulette. . . . There is also the fact that the gambling scenes take place at a foreign resort and the story deals with an expatriate Russian. This, although a detail, is quite important nevertheless. . . . Possibly this novel will be a very good one. . . . It is a description of a sort of hell [the gaming rooms] of the same type as that bath-house scene at the penal settlement [in *The House of the Dead*], and I will do my best to present it all in a very striking form.

It was not until after three years, two deaths, and many disastrous sessions at the green tables that Dostoevsky realized this project.

By that time he had to produce it or face disastrous consequences: all his writings would become the property of the unscrupulous publisher Stelovsky unless *The Gambler* was delivered by November 1, 1866.

On October 1, Dostoevsky hadn't yet written a word (he was busy working on *Crime and Punishment,* contracted for by another publisher) and he was on the verge of despair—he couldn't possibly meet the deadline, and would face financial disaster.

However, he was saved by his friend Miliukov, who recommended to him a pretty young secretary, the daughter of a friend of his, and an expert at taking shorthand. This was Anna Grigorievna Snitkina, who was to become Dostoevsky's second wife. He dictated to her the story of a gambler that he had carried in him for so long. They were through before the deadline and the manuscript was deposited and registered at the police station, since the wily Stelovsky had deliberately absented himself from town to make delivery impossible.

And after that, Dostoevsky enjoyed a happy marriage. Anna proved to be not only an excellent stenographer, but also an efficient business woman who straightened out his affairs, and a loving wife.

All this, however, did not prevent Dostoevsky from continuing to gamble. Once, while they were abroad, fleeing their creditors, Dostoevsky left his wife in Dresden, a town quite strange to her, and went, with her consent, to Homburg to have another go at roulette and retrieve their finances, which were out of hand again.

A few days later he wrote to her:

. . . I started to play first thing in the morning and by noon I was a hundred gulden down. After lunch I returned to the casino, having firmly promised myself to be as reasonable as possible and, thank God, I recuperated all the morning's losses and won a hundred more. I could have left with a net gain of three hundred gulden, for at one point I held them in my hand. However, I played them and lost. Now listen to what I have drawn from this, Annette: provided you are reasonable and have a head made of marble, cool and superhumanly cautious, there is not the slightest doubt that you can win anything you wish. And so I shall expend great effort to think and keep control. . . .

But on the following day he writes:

I have lost much more than I could afford to. I shouldn't really gamble with my weak nerves. . . . Tonight I will have a last try with what I have left—which is a mere drop. . . .

And he loses again. He still repeats in his letters to his wife that "it is quite impossible to lose if you play coolly, using your head," but he offers an alibi: he was too anxious, in too much of a hurry to win and return to her, and so he couldn't be sufficiently detached. Please, could she send him some money for his trip back.

She did, and went to the station to meet the train that was supposed to bring him back. But he wasn't on it. The next day she received a letter which began: "Anna, my dearest, my darling wife, please forgive me and don't dismiss me as a good-for-nothing. I have lost everything you sent me, everything, down to the last pfennig. . . ."

He again asks her to send him his fare and this time is on the train. But this is still not the end.

After they had received some money from a publisher, Dostoevsky decided to move to Baden-Baden. His gambling went on and on. He even reached a point where he left his wife penniless and pregnant in a hotel room and went out with the proceeds from pawning her earrings to "try and catch up."

He borrowed money from everyone he could think of, including Turgenev, whom he hated (he asked him for a hundred thalers, and Turgenev let him have fifty).

And so, Dostoevsky continued to indulge his lust for roulette, an indulgence which resulted in nausea and despair, in self-deprecation and promises that he was through with gambling. But he broke his vows every time, until April 28, 1871. That day he wrote to his wife, after having lost the rescue money she'd just sent him: "Anna, Anna, you must understand that I am not just an unscrupulous creature—I am a man devoured by the passion for gambling. But I want you to know that now that mirage has been dispersed once and for all and I feel I have been released from this delusion. . . ."

And, true enough, he never gambled again. That was almost five years after he had written *The Gambler,* about eight years after he had conceived the idea of the novel.

Thus *The Gambler* was dictated by Dostoevsky to his future second wife, after his passion for Apollinaria Suslova had been pretty much spent, but while his passion for gambling was still extremely virulent. Indeed, when the worst was yet to come.

And so the man who reeled off the story to the efficient and admiring Anna, to whom he was about to declare his love, was no longer quite the same man as the miserable, rejected lover who spent his nights in the casino at least partly to make up for his frustrations. When he wrote to Strakhov giving the outline for his future novel, the book he had in mind was quite different from what was later to be so quickly and strangely produced, and it is rather surprising that so many literary analysts elect to analyze that outline rather than to look into the novel itself to see what Dostoevsky thought and meant when he actually dictated it.

To point out just one difference—the central character as outlined by Dostoevsky in his letter to Strakhov resembled the author much more than Alexei. There is no evidence one way or the other that Alexei has lost his faith without daring to become an atheist, nor that "it makes him feel better to think that there is nothing for him to do in Russia." But much more important: in the outline, Dostoevsky's hero slips into the habit of gambling in which he wastes his talents *for three years* and then is apparently redeemed; the actual novel ends on a note of damnation— he will quit as soon as he gets even, when he catches up, and the obvious implication is that that day will never come.

The Gambler as it stands is much less autobiographical than Dostoevsky had conceived it three years before it was written. During that painful trip with Suslova, feeling humiliated and inadequate both in her company and at the gambling table, it would seem that Dostoevsky was trying to "explain" how such a *déchéance* was possible (lack of faith, loss of contact with one's native soil; there is no mention of a woman in the outline). Later, looking at it in retrospect, he changed the central character considerably and introduced as a co-star Paulina (a woman only partly based on Suslova), for whom Alexei's love is not at all as total as he at first imagined. (Suslova's sway over Dostoevsky was broken by then.)

Indeed, Dostoevsky must have thoroughly reworked in his head the novel he was to dictate in such a hurry, for *The Gambler* is uncannily well composed. As usual, Dostoevsky is seething with ideas, observations, descriptions, and opinions, seemingly thrown in with abandon, but actually fitted nicely into a harmonious composition which shows once more what a "natural" novelist he was.

The Gambler would stand as a success even taken only as a portrait of a young man who became addicted to gambling, a passion for which he seems to have been predestined by birth. As this is happening to him, the freaks, the flunkeys, the cranks, the chips of international flotsam, all drift in and out before our eyes, while we also receive a technical explanation of roulette and a rather cockeyed, metaphysical view on probabilities.

But, of course, there is much more to it than that.

Alexei, like so many other characters in Dostoevsky's novels, is trying to break through the wall of the established order and the human condition itself. In *Crime and Punishment*, Raskolnikov tries to break through it by killing; in *The Adolescent*, the hero tries to climb over it by becoming "not simply rich, but rich as Rothschild"; and in *The Possessed*, various characters try to raze it, by political action, suicide, gratuitous acts, and what not. Like them, Alexei feels that ordinary human emotions and passions (including love) fall short of something and cannot therefore be ends in themselves. And he finds in gambling a path that will take him beyond them, but which, alas, leads him to an impasse.

In this novel about games of chance, gambling spreads well beyond the green tables of the casino. It is like a strain of music to which all the characters of the book dance. The stakes are love or money, or both.

As the story begins, three characters—the General, Alexei, and Paulina—are all desperately in love: the General with Blanche; Alexei with Paulina; and Paulina with Des Grieux. Each of them stakes everything to achieve his aim, and they all lose: the "Grandmother" from whom the General hopes to inherit refuses to die; Paulina's "gift of herself" to Des Grieux fails to light a spark of comparable passion in him; Alexei, instead of mastering probabilities, is sucked into the whirl caused by the roulette wheel. And having lost, the three protagonists slither to their *déchéance*: the General, who had aspired to possess Blanche completely, settles, after his stroke, for an occasional pat or two on the head from her; Paulina, the idealist, settles for a dull, respectable life; Alexei, who had aspired to win millions, is happy now when he gains a few gulden for his dinner and lives on the mere hope of "breaking even."

Both the leading lady and the leading man are fierce idealists, although, of course, like all Dostoevsky's characters, they are completely misguided—the author himself is merely groping for an answer.

The fictional Paulina, a pure romantic, is taken in by the superficial French polish of Des Grieux (named, no doubt, for Manon Lescaut's pimpish lover), gambles her virtue and reputation and "gives herself" to him, feeling he will understand if he is really the romantic hero she believes him to be. When it turns out that he is not, she comes to "give herself" to Alexei, who, instead of taking her in his arms, rushes out to win enough money at roulette to refund to the original villain his investment in the lady (some fifty thousand francs). In the course of winning, Alexei realizes that if he had to choose between Paulina and roulette, he would pick roulette. Thus the moment at which Paulina and Alexei come closest to realizing their love goes by, and the scene in Alexei's hotel room is one of literature's many "brief encounters"—they pass each other like two passengers in different trains that stop briefly at a station. And it is only as the trains start moving in opposite directions and the rhythmical rumble of motion sets in that they reach out desperately for each other.

Afterward, mortified by Alexei's lack of understanding, Paulina rushes off to the Hotel d'Angleterre suite occupied by Astley, the honorable, intelligent, stiff-necked, and (very important) non-gambling Englishman—he just watches. He loves her too, even understands her, but prosaic as he is, can offer her only comfortable and respectable shelter instead of the romantic, all-transcending feeling that she is seeking.

Thus, in the course of the book, the idealistic young Paulina is seen hopping from one man's arms to another's, just like the venal Blanche, although, of course, for very different reasons. The final score—three each.

The narrator of the story, Alexei, often naively taken as Dostoevsky's alter ego, is really very different from his creator. He is a born, predestined gambler, long before he even gets around to putting down his first stake. He always plays all or nothing. At the beginning of the story, for instance, he defies the social hierarchy, speaking out of order at the table and risking not only his job (he could find himself penniless abroad) but also the possibility of staying close to the woman he loves, and all that just to gain a mere acknowledgment of his existence. And then again, he is willing to jump from the Schlangenberg for the sake of his love, or to insult the Baroness (as he complies with that whim he has, significantly, a sensation of falling), although such exploits could hardly win him Paulina's love. This is very important because it brings out the element of irrationality inherent in gambling which, Dostoevsky shows, is also a perversion of idealism.

The point made very strongly in *The Gambler* is that real gambling begins only when *everything* is at stake. Only when he himself reached that point of crisis did Alexei, like Dostoevsky, realize that he loved gambling for its own sake, and not as a means of saving a hopeless financial situation.

But even after a real gambler has realized that, a curious

11

mechanism in him sets into motion to obliterate this awareness the moment the sickening aftertaste of the latest disaster vanishes. And so, a few days, sometimes only a few hours, after having been moaning and swearing off, promising that he would never, never again . . . Anna had to listen to heated tirades about the *inevitability* of the triumph of a man over the roulette ball, provided, of course, he had a cool head and the strength of will. And he would believe it until the next catastrophe.

It may be of interest at this point to take a look at Freud's interpretation of Dostoevsky's passion for gambling in his essay, "Dostoyevsky and Parricide." Freud asserts that gambling in Dostoevsky was "a form of self-punishment" and that he enjoyed abasing himself in a flood of contrition before his young wife after losing money. From there, Freud goes on to analyze not Dostoevsky's *The Gambler* but a short story by Stefan Zweig. In a long digression, he seeks to establish through that story that the gambling urge is in reality a "repetition of the onanism compulsion." And, despite Zweig's specific denial that his character was a latent onanist (dismissed since the author may be unaware of his creation's subconscious twists), Freud goes on to say:

> If the gambling habit, with its unsuccessful struggles to break oneself from it and its opportunities for self-punishment, is a repetition of the onanism compulsion, we shall not be surprised that it gained such a firm place in Dostoyevsky's life. We find no case of serious neurosis in which the autoerotic satisfaction of immaturity and puberty does not play its part, and the relations between the effort to suppress it and the fear of the father are so well known that they need only be mentioned.

Of course, one can easily visualize Dostoevsky exasperated by Suslova's rejection (she wouldn't allow him to touch her during their trip), rushing to the nearest casino and gambling there until morning. In this case the substitution would seem much more direct (without going through poor Stefan Zweig). But even so, Dostoevsky obligingly offers us a control experiment which forces us to discard such a glib solution—he went on rushing off to the casino even when he was very happily married to Anna Grigorievna (with whom he had four children).

The answer, of course, lies in the complexity of human nature, in which gambling may represent different things to different persons, although, again, one can make anything out of it one wants. In Dostoevsky, for instance, the exalted craving for gambling was regularly succeeded by a state of dejection and disgust that could easily be compared to certain states of post-detumescence, but not more so than to the feeling of the "morning after" following a night of drunkenness, or simply the new stark realization of the hopelessness of his material situation coming after a delusion of escaping quickly from that misery.

As a matter of fact, the difference in different people's attitudes toward gambling is shown beautifully in *The Gambler* by the most forceful character of the book—the Grandmother. She comes, gambles with passion, loses, and leaves. She can do so because she has roots in the world— she is a Russian, in the Dostoevskian sense of the word, she *belongs,* and gambling is only a crazy escapade to her. She enjoys it, gets scratched, and goes back to what she still owns, which is plenty.

Dostoevsky himself, unlike his Alexei, gave up gambling. There were other things more important to him— his writing, for one. And so, in a way, Dostoevsky's gambling is more like the Grandmother's than Alexei's or any of his other characters', or even that of Stefan Zweig's young man from Monte Carlo.

But then, maybe the poor, paralyzed old lady was also punishing herself.

Besides Freud's, there are many possible explanations. A Marxist critic might suggest, for instance, that both the Grandmother and Alexei represent decaying capitalism, with Alexei at a more advanced stage of disintegration. Indeed, any believer in a one-track-minded providence might tailor to his pet system an explanation of what made the author and his characters tick. But Dostoevsky, thank God, had a complex, untidy, questioning view of the universe. If he hadn't, he could never have introduced such a highly whimsical, unpredictable providence into the background of his novels, and his people would not come bursting upon us as they do.

And that goes for *The Gambler* too.

Andrew R. MacAndrew
University of Virginia

THE GAMBLER

I

At last I was back after my two weeks' absence. The others had been in Roulettenburg for three days already. I had expected them to be waiting impatiently for me, but I was wrong. The General looked at me casually, said a few condescending words, and sent me off to his sister. It was obvious that they had managed to get their hands on some cash. In fact, the General seemed positively embarrassed to look me in the face. Maria Filipovna was extremely busy; however, she exchanged a few indifferent words with me, accepted the money, counted it, and heard out my report. They were expecting Mezentsov to lunch, and also a little Frenchman and some Englishman or other. Now that there was money, we couldn't do without a luncheon party—Moscow fashion.

When Paulina saw me she asked why I had been away so long, and then walked off without waiting for an answer. Obviously, she did so deliberately. Nevertheless, I feel we must have it out. Too many things have accumulated.

They put me in a small room on the fourth floor of the hotel. They were well aware that I was part of the General's retinue. Everything indicated that our group had already caught the public eye. Everyone was under the impression that the General was a prominent Russian of tremendous wealth. Even before lunch, he managed, among other errands, to give me two thousand-franc notes to change. I had them changed at the hotel desk. Now we will pass for millionaires here for at least a week.

I was going to take Misha and Nadia for a walk, and was already downstairs when the General summoned me—he suddenly wanted to know where I was going to take the children.

The man simply cannot look me straight in the eye, although I'm sure he wishes he could. But each time he tries I meet his look with a straight—that is, arrogant—stare that seems to make him feel ill at ease.

In very pompous language, slapping one phrase on top of the other and finally getting completely mixed up, he intimated that I must take the children to the park and stay as far away as possible from the Casino. In the end, he lost his temper and said abruptly:

"Otherwise you are likely to take them into the Casino, to the roulette table! Well," he added, "you must excuse me, but you are still rather irresponsible, and I know how strongly gambling attracts you. . . . In any case, I am not your mentor, nor do I wish to act as such, but I have the right, at least, to demand that you should not compromise me. . . ."

"But I don't even have any money," I said quietly. "One has to have money if one is to lose it."

"As to that, I'll pay you right away," the General said.

He flushed slightly, searched for something in the drawers of his desk, checked something in his notebook. It turned out that he owed me about a hundred and twenty rubles.

"Well, what are we going to do?" the General went on. "We must calculate how much it would be in thalers. . . . Here, take a hundred thalers, to make a round figure, and you may rest assured you won't lose the balance, whatever it is."

I accepted the money in silence.

"And, please, you mustn't resent what I have said. You are much too touchy. I merely meant to warn you, so to speak, with that remark, and, of course, I have a certain right to do that. . . ."

Returning home with the children before lunch, I met a whole cavalcade: our crowd had driven out to visit some ruins. There were two fine carriages with beautiful horses. In one carriage sat Mademoiselle Blanche with Maria Filipovna and Paulina. The General, the little Frenchman, and the Englishman were on horseback. The people in the street stopped and stared. The desired effect was produced. But I reckoned the General was in trouble: with the four thousand francs I had brought with me, plus the money they had managed to lay their hands on here, they must have, say, seven or eight thousand francs—and that won't be enough to tempt Mademoiselle Blanche.

Mademoiselle Blanche and her mother are also staying in our hotel. And our Frenchie has a room here somewhere too. The waiters call him "Monsieur le Comte," and Mademoiselle Blanche's mother, "Madame la Comtesse." Well, who knows, perhaps they really are *comte* and *comtesse.*

I knew in advance that Monsieur le Comte wouldn't recognize me when we met at lunch. Of course, it never even occurred to the General to introduce us, or even to present me to him. Monsieur le Comte has been to Russia himself and knows what an unimportant creature a tutor is. But in reality, he knows me very well indeed.

To tell the truth, I had come to lunch uninvited; I believe the General had forgotten all about me, for otherwise I'm sure he would have sent me to have my lunch at the *table d'hôte.* I had come on my own initiative, and the General gave me a disapproving look. But the kindly Maria Filipovna pointed out a chair for me. Then, the fact that I had met Mr. Astley before saved me from further embarrassment and, whether they liked it or not, I was now one of the company.

I had met that strange Englishman in a railway carriage in Prussia, when I was on my way to join our party. We had sat opposite each other. Then I met him again when we were crossing the French border, and later again in Switzerland—twice within a couple of weeks. And now, here he was again, in Roulettenburg.

Never in my life had I met a shyer man. He was morbidly shy and was well aware of it, because he wasn't at all stupid. In general, he is a very nice, quiet person. I got him talking the first time we met in Prussia. He told me that he had been to the North Cape that summer and that he would have liked very much to attend the Nizhni-Novgorod fair. I don't know how he became acquainted with the General. I am under the impression that he is desperately in love with Paulina. He turned bright red when she came in. He seemed delighted when I sat down next to him at the table, and he treated me like a bosom friend.

During lunch, the Frenchie showed off unabashedly, treating everyone with stuffy condescension. I remembered how, back in Moscow too, he used to put on grand airs. He spoke a great deal about finance and about Russian politics. From time to time the General dared to disagree with him, but he did so very quietly, and only to maintain his authority.

I was in a strange mood. It goes without saying that well before lunch was halfway through I had managed to ask myself the eternal question: Why was I still trailing after the General; why hadn't I broken with these people long ago?

Now and then I stole a glance at Paulina. She took no notice of me whatsoever. Finally, I became furious and decided to be rude.

Suddenly, and without the slightest provocation, I loudly broke into the others' conversation. I wanted above all to pick a quarrel with the Frenchman. I turned to the General and very loudly and clearly—interrupting him, I believe—pointed out that this summer it was almost impossible for Russians to dine at the *table d'hôte* in hotels. The General stared at me in surprise.

"If you happen to be a self-respecting person," I went on, "you'll be shocked and feel personally insulted. In Paris and on the Rhine, even in Switzerland, there are swarms of those little Poles at the *table d'hôte,* and also Frenchmen who are in sympathy with them, so that if you happen to be a Russian you don't get a chance to say a word."

I said it in French. The General looked at me non-plused, wondering whether he should be angry, or merely content himself with being surprised that I could lose my temper to such an extent.

"I suppose someone somewhere has given you a lesson in good behavior," the Frenchman said with bored contempt.

"In Paris," I said, "I got into a row with a Pole and then with a French officer who came to the Pole's assistance. But then, some other Frenchmen sided with me when I told them that I had threatened to spit into a Monsignor's coffee."

"Spit?" the General asked in solemn disapproval, looking around him.

The Frenchman looked me up and down incredulously.

"It's just as I said," I replied. "As I was quite certain I'd have to go to Rome on our business, I went to the chancellery of the nuncio of the Holy See in Paris to get a visa stamped on my passport. I was received there by a priest of about fifty or so, a small dry man with frost in his face. He heard me out politely but very coldly and asked me to wait. And although I didn't have much time, I sat down and waited. I picked up an *Opinion Nationale,* in which I read some most insulting stuff about Russia. And as I was reading I noticed someone pass into the Monsignor's room. I looked up and saw my priest ushering him in with a bow. So I repeated my request and he again asked me to wait, this time in an even drier tone. After a while, somebody I hadn't seen before, but who was obviously on business, entered the waiting room. I believe he was an Austrian. Well, he was ushered in immediately. That made me very angry. I stood up, walked over to the priest, and in a very firm tone told him that, since the Monsignor was receiving, he could perhaps attend to me now. The priest drew back from me with a stunned look on his face. It was simply beyond him—how could an insignificant Russian possibly put himself on the same plane with the Monsignor's guests? He looked me up and down with the utmost insolence, obviously delighted to have an opportunity to humble me, and shouted:

" 'Do you really imagine that Monsignor is going to leave his coffee for your sake?'

"Then I began to shout even louder than he:

" 'Let me tell you that I spit in your Monsignor's coffee! And if you don't attend to my passport this very second, I'll go and see him myself!'

" 'What do you mean?' the priest screamed. 'You'd go in while there is a cardinal sitting in his office?'

"He shrank back from me in horror, darted to the door, spread out his arms, and put on an expression that signified that he'd rather die than let me in.

"So I told him that I was a heretic and a barbarian—*un hérétique et un barbare*—and that I couldn't care less about his archbishops, cardinals, monsignors, *et al*. In brief, I showed him that I wasn't going to give up. He looked at me with infinite hatred, then snatched the passport out of my hand, and took it upstairs. A minute later, it had the visa on it. Here, would you like to have a look?"

I took out the passport and showed them the papal visa.

"But still, I must say . . ." the General muttered.

"What saved you was your declaration that you were a barbarian and a heretic," the Frenchman sneered. *"Cela n'était pas si bête."*

"But should we Russians accept such treatment? Should we just sit there and listen without daring to protest, and even be prepared to renounce our country? In Paris, at least, people in my hotel started to treat me with greater respect when I told them about my fight with the priest. The fat Pole who had been the most hostile to me at the *table d'hôte* faded into the background at once. And the Frenchmen listened without protest when I told them that a couple of years before I had met a person at whom a French soldier had fired in 1812 just for the sake of discharging his rifle. At the time, that person was a ten-year-old child whose family hadn't been able to get out of Moscow in time."

"That's impossible!" the Frenchie said, losing his temper. "A French soldier would never fire at a child."

"Nevertheless, he did," I said. "That incident was related to me by a highly respected retired army captain, and I myself saw the scar the bullet had left on his cheek."

The Frenchman began to speak very fast, and at great length. The General tried to support him. But I advised him to read the memoirs of General Petrovsky, who was a prisoner of war of the French in 1812. At last Maria Filipovna started to say something, just to interrupt our argument. The General was extremely displeased with me, because by then both the Frenchman and I were shouting at the tops of our voices. But I believe Mr. Astley greatly enjoyed my argument with the Frenchman, for when we were leaving the table he suggested that he and I have a drink of wine together.

In the evening, I managed to have a fifteen-minute talk with Paulina. Our exchange took place during a stroll. We had all gone out into the park and were walking toward the Casino. Paulina sat down on a bench facing the fountain and let Nadia play at a little distance with some other children. I, too, allowed Misha to walk off toward the fountain, and at last we were alone.

Of course we started to talk business. Paulina was quite angry when I handed her only seven hundred gulden. She had expected me to bring her at least two thousand from Paris, which she had thought I could get by pawning her jewels.

"I must have that money, come what may," she said. "We must get it, or I'm lost."

I started questioning her about what had happened while I was away.

"Nothing, except the two reports from Petersburg: first, that Grandmother was very ill; and then, two days later, that she must have died already. That report came through Timofei Petrovich," Paulina added, "and he is a very reliable man. Now we are waiting for final, definite confirmation."

23

"And so everyone's holding his breath in expectation?"

"Of course everyone is. For the past six months that has been the only hope . . ."

"And you too were reckoning on it?"

"Why, I'm no relative of hers. I am only the General's stepdaughter. Nevertheless, I am quite convinced that she won't have forgotten me in her will."

"I am under the impression that you'll get plenty," I said with assurance.

"Well, as a matter of fact, she was quite fond of me. But why should *you* be so sure of it?"

"Tell me," I said to her instead of answering; "it seems our marquis is also quite up to date on all the family secrets?"

"And you yourself, why should you be interested in it all?" Paulina asked, giving me a stern look.

"And I say he has good reasons to be interested," I said, "because, unless I am mistaken, the General has already borrowed some money from him."

"Your assumption is quite correct."

"Well, do you imagine he would have advanced money if he hadn't known about the old lady? Didn't you notice that he mentioned the Grandmother three times at the table, always referring to her as 'Grandma.' What intimate and familiar ways!"

"Yes, you're right there. As soon as he found out that I was mentioned in the will, too, he immediately started taking an interest in me. Is that what you were trying to find out?"

"Has he just now started taking an interest in you? I thought he had done so for a long time."

"You know very well that that's not true," Paulina said angrily. After a pause she inquired: "And where did you meet that Englishman?"

"I knew you were going to ask me about him."

I told her about my former meetings with Mr. Astley during my travels.

"He is shy, and prone to fall in love," I said, "and probably he's already in love with you."

"Yes, he's in love with me."

"And there's no doubt that he is ten times as wealthy as the Frenchman. Tell me, is it certain that the Frenchman has money? Isn't it doubtful?"

"No doubt about it at all. He has a château. Only yesterday the General told me that for a fact. Well, are you satisfied now?"

"If I were you I would marry the Englishman."

"Why?" Paulina asked.

"The Frenchman is better-looking, but he is a despicable man. The Englishman is not only honest—he is ten times richer on top of that."

"Yes, but then the Frenchman—the Marquis—is more intelligent," she said in the most matter-of-fact tone.

"Are you so sure of that?" I said in the same tone.

"I am."

My questions irritated Paulina very much, and I saw that she was trying to enrage me by her tone and by the incongruity of her answers. And I immediately told her so.

"Well, it really would amuse me to see you in a rage. That's the only reason why I've allowed you to ask me such questions and make such assumptions. And now you ought to pay for it."

"Well, it's quite true that I think I can afford to ask you such questions, because I am prepared to pay any price for them, and I feel my life is worth nothing now."

Paulina laughed.

"Last time, on the Schlangenberg, you told me that if I said the word, you would be prepared to dive head first from the cliff, which, I believe, is over a thousand feet high. Well, some day I'll say the word, just to see how you pay off. And rest assured—I'll have the strength of character to go through with it. I loathe you especially because I have allowed you so much, and I loathe you even more because I need you so badly. So, as long as I need you, I am forced to spare your life."

She stood up. She had spoken with irritation. Lately she has always ended our conversations in irritation and hatred —yes, real hatred.

"May I inquire who this Mademoiselle Blanche is?" I asked her, unwilling to let her leave without an explanation.

"You know yourself who she is. Nothing new has been added since then. It looks as if Mademoiselle Blanche will wind up as the General's wife. Provided, of course, that the rumor about Grandmother's death is confirmed; for otherwise, Mademoiselle Blanche, her mama, and her distant relative *le marquis*—the lot of them—are very well aware that we are broke."

"And what about the General? Is he hopelessly in love?"

"That's not what matters most now. Listen, and remember well: take these seven hundred florins and go and play roulette with them. Win as much as you can for me —I must get the money now at all costs."

With that, she called Nadia and walked off in the direction of the Casino, near which she joined the rest of our party. I turned into the first path that appeared on my left, thinking hard and wondering. It was as if I had received a blow on the head when she ordered me to the roulette table. It was strange—there was plenty to make me stop and think, but instead I plunged into an analysis of my feelings for Paulina. I certainly had felt easier during my two weeks' absence than on the day of my return here, although I had missed her madly during my travels, and had even kept seeing her in my mind's eye. Once— I believe in a railway carriage in Switzerland—I had dozed off and in my sleep had spoken to Paulina, which made the people in my compartment laugh. And now, once again, I asked myself the question: Do I love her? And once again, I was unable to answer it, that is, I said to myself for the hundredth time: I hate her. Yes, she is loathsome to me. There have been moments (especially toward the end of our talks) when I would have given half my life to strangle her. I swear that if it had been possible to press a sharp knife slowly into her breast, I think I would have done it with delight. But at the same time, I swear by everything that is sacred to me that if, on the Schlangenberg cliff, she had really asked me to

26

jump, I'd have done so without the least hesitation, even joyfully. I knew it.

Anyway, one way or another, the thing was going to end. She understood that very well, and I realized quite clearly how inaccessible she was for me, how impossible was the realization of my dreams, while she was well aware that I realized it and, I am sure, enjoyed the idea very much; for otherwise, how could a clever and cautious person like her be so open and frank with me? I believe she felt like that empress of ancient times who undressed in front of her slave because, to her, he wasn't a human being. And often, I wasn't a human being to Paulina either.

Nevertheless, I had her command—to win at roulette at all costs. There was no time for me to ask myself why she needed the money, why she was in such a hurry, and what new schemes she was hatching in that ever busy head of hers. Besides, in the past two weeks many new facts of which I had no inkling must obviously have come to complicate things. I had to find it all out, to penetrate all those secrets, and the sooner the better. But for the moment, I had no time—I had to get to the roulette table.

II

I admit I didn't like it. Although I'd made up my mind to play, I felt reluctant to stand in for someone else. It had me quite upset, and I approached the roulette table with a very unpleasant feeling. And when I looked around I didn't like what I saw.

I never could stand the flunkeyish attitude adopted by the press in general and by our Russian newspapers in particular, when, each spring, they expatiate on two aspects of gambling: one, the incredible splendor and magnificence of the casinos in the roulette towns on the Rhine; and two, the gold that is supposed to be piled on the tables. I am sure the reporters are not paid to write that stuff, but that they do it out of sheer disinterested servility. No, there is no splendor whatsoever in those sordid rooms, and as to gold, not only is it not piled on the tables, but one scarcely ever catches sight of it. Of course, it is possible that at one point in the course of the season, there may materialize a crank, or some Englishman, or maybe an Oriental of some sort or other, or perhaps a Turk, as happened this summer, who will proceed to win or lose very large sums; but the rest play for quite low stakes, and on an average day there is very little money lying on the table.

When I walked into the gaming room—it was the first time in my life—I didn't dare to play for a while. Besides, I felt crowded. Although, even if I had been there all alone, even then I think I would have walked off without playing. I confess that my heart was pounding in my breast and that I didn't feel at all cool and detached; probably I had felt for a long time already that I would leave Roulettenburg a different man and that something was about to happen which would radically and irrevocably change my life. I felt that it was bound to happen. Although it may seem ridiculous to say that I expected so much from roulette, I find the generally accepted opinion that it is stupid to expect anything from gambling even more ridiculous. And why should gambling be considered worse than any other way of getting money, such as commerce, for instance? It's true, of course, that out of a hundred persons who play roulette, perhaps one winds up a winner. But why should I care about that?

In any case, I decided to watch the game first, and not to try anything serious that night. That evening, even if something were to happen, it would be accidental and unimportant—that was what I had decided. And then I had to study the game itself, for despite the thousands of descriptions of roulette I had read, always with great eagerness, I could know nothing about the mechanics of it until I watched the game myself.

At first, the whole thing seemed, in a way, dirty to me

—somehow morally wrong, and unclean. And here, I do not mean at all the worried and greedy faces that cluster in dozens or even in hundreds around the gambling table. I see absolutely nothing wrong in wanting to win quickly as much money as possible. I have always dismissed as very stupid the idea of that smug and well-off moralist who, in answering someone's excuse that people in general play for small stakes, said that that made it even worse because it revealed that even their greed was petty. As if it mattered whether greed was big or little! That is simply a matter of proportion. Something that is very small for Rothschild is enormous for me, and as to the gain or profit, it is not only at the roulette table that people keep winning and snatching things away from one another. Now, whether gain and profit are despicable things is another question. And I am not going to try to answer it here.

Anyway, since I was myself extremely eager to win, all that greed, repulsive though it may have been, seemed rather congenial and understandable as I walked into the room. It is very nice when people stop putting up a front before one another and start acting frankly and openly. And why should one deceive oneself? It is the most futile and unprofitable pastime. What struck me as very unprepossessing at first was the seriousness, even respect, for their occupation that roulette-playing scum displayed as they stepped up to the tables. And that is why such a sharp distinction is drawn between the style of gambling branded as *mauvais genre* and the gambling in which a self-respecting person may indulge. There are two sorts of gambling, one for gentlemen and the other for plebeians—the scum plays for profit. Here, this difference is very strongly emphasized. Yet, in its essence, the differentiation is really very offensive.

A gentleman, for instance, may stake five or ten louis d'or, but hardly ever much more, although if he is really very rich, he may even stake a thousand francs; but whatever it is, he does it merely for sport's sake, just to have a bit of fun, just to experience the sensation of winning or losing, but under no circumstances must he be preoc-cupied by the sum itself that he is trying to win. If he wins, he may, for instance, burst into loud laughter or make some amusing comment to a neighbor, or he can stake the whole thing again and even double it; but he may only do so out of curiosity, just to experiment with probabilities, and never for the sake of a plebeian preoc-cupation with gain. In brief, a gentleman must view all the gaming tables, all roulette and *trente et quarante* as merely a sport organized exclusively for his enjoyment. He is not even allowed to suspect the lures and traps on which gambling is based. And it would be very desirable indeed for him to believe that all the other gamblers, all the scum around the tables, trembling over one gulden, were wealthy gentlemen like himself, also playing just for fun. Such complete ignorance of the facts and such in-nocence of outlook would certainly be considered very aristocratic. I have seen many respectable mothers thrust-ing a few gold coins into the hands of their fifteen- or sixteen-year-old daughters, pushing them forward toward the gaming tables and teaching them how to play. Win or lose, the young lady unfailingly smiles and walks away very pleased with herself.

Our General walked up to the table with great decorum. A flunkey picked up a chair and hurried over to offer it to him, but the General never even noticed the servant. He stood there, very slowly taking out his purse and then, also very slowly, taking three hundred francs in gold out of it and putting them on the black. The black won. He didn't pick up his winnings, but left them on the table. The black won again. He left them again. And when the red won that time, he lost twelve hundred francs in one go. He smiled and walked away with perfect control. I am convinced that black cats were clawing at his heart, and that if the stake had been twice or perhaps three times greater, he would have lost control and showed his agita-tion.

On the other hand, I once saw a Frenchman winning and then losing something like thirty thousand francs without showing a sign of emotion. A true gentleman must remain unruffled even if he loses his whole fortune. Money must be so much less important than good manners that it isn't worth bothering about.

It is, of course, very aristocratic to ignòre completely the surrounding scum and the sordidness. At times, however, the opposite may be equally aristocratic—a gentleman may take notice of his surroundings, may examine them closely, even through a lorgnette, as long as he views this scum and squalor as a source of entertainment, like a show organized especially for the amusement of gentlemen. So it becomes permissible for him to mingle with the crowd as long as he convinces himself that he is only a spectator and in no way a part of it. But then, he shouldn't really look at things too closely, for that would be rather ungentlemanly, since the spectacle is certainly not worth the close attention of a gentleman.

But for my part, I thought it was worth a very close look, especially as I had come there not merely as an observer, but considering myself honestly and frankly as one of the rabble. As to my deep personal moral views, they, of course, have no place in the present discussion. Let us take it for granted, then, that I am saying all this to relieve my conscience. But let me say this: lately I have felt very averse to evaluating my acts and my thoughts by any moral standards. I have been governed by something else.

As to the mob, their way of gambling is really quite repulsive. I wouldn't even mind saying that a lot of plain stealing goes on around the table. It is very hard on the croupiers, who sit at the ends of the tables, watch the stakes, collect the money, and make the pay-offs. And they, too, are a quite unsavory lot. Mostly French. . . .

But really, I have not made all these observations and remarks just to describe roulette—I am trying to get my own bearings, so that I'll know how to behave in the future myself. I have noticed that there is nothing too surprising about some hand shooting out from under the table and grabbing your winnings. That usually starts an argument; sometimes there's shouting, and then witnesses must be found to establish that the stake was yours in the first place.

At first the whole thing was a sort of Chinese puzzle to me; I simply guessed, managing somehow to observe that stakes could be placed on individual numbers, on "odds or evens," and on the colors. That evening I decided to risk one hundred gulden of Paulina's money. The thought that I was to gamble for someone else confused me. It was a very unpleasant feeling that I tried to stifle. I couldn't get rid of the impression that, in starting to gamble for Paulina, I was going to wreck my own life. Is it really possible to touch a roulette table without becoming contaminated with superstition?

I began by taking our fifty gulden and placing them on "evens." The wheel spun, and stopped on the number thirteen. I had lost. Feeling rather sick, and now only trying to get rid of the rest of the hundred gulden and leave, I put the remaining fifty on the red. The red came up. I left the hundred gulden where they were and the red came up again. Again I stuck to the same color, and the red won once more. I picked up the four hundred gulden and placed two hundred of them on the set of twelve middle figures, without the slightest idea what would come of it. They paid me three times my stake. So the original one hundred gulden I had had in my hand had suddenly become eight hundred. All at once a strange sensation made things so unbearable for me that I decided I'd have to leave. I felt that if I had been playing for myself I wouldn't have played that way at all. Nevertheless, I placed all eight hundred gulden on evens. Number four came up and they counted out another eight hundred for me. Then I picked up the pile of sixteen hundred gulden and went to look for Paulina.

They had all gone out and were walking somewhere in the park, so I only saw her at dinner. This time, the Frenchman was not there, and the General let himself go. Among other things, he felt it was appropriate for him to remark once more that he didn't like to see me at the roulette table. He said it could be embarrassing for him if I lost too badly.

"And even if you won a great deal," he said, "it would also be embarrassing for me. Of course," he added with a significant look, "I have no right to dictate your conduct to you, but you must understand yourself . . ."

And, as was his habit, he didn't finish.

I replied drily that I had very little money, and that it would hardly be very conspicuous even if I lost everything.

When I went upstairs, I handed Paulina the money I had won for her and told her that I would never gamble on her behalf again.

"Why is that?" she asked, alarmed.

"Because I intend to play for myself, and that prevents it," I answered, looking at her in surprise.

"So you are still convinced that roulette is the only solution and salvation you have left?" she asked me sarcastically.

I answered in a serious tone, "Yes"; and as to my feeling of assurance that I would win, it might be very funny, but I would greatly appreciate it if she would leave me in peace.

Paulina tried to insist that I share that day's proceeds with her fifty-fifty. She handed me eight hundred gulden and suggested that henceforward we continue on that basis. I refused the half of the proceeds categorically, and told her that I couldn't play on behalf of others, not because I didn't want to but because I was certain to lose that way.

"But, stupid as it may sound," she said, growing dreamy, "I too have all my hopes staked on roulette. And so you must go on gambling on a fifty-fifty basis with me, and of course you will."

And she walked away without listening to my further protests.

III.

However, yesterday she didn't say a word to me about gambling. As a matter of fact, she avoided addressing me altogether. Her former attitude toward me didn't change, though. She still treated me in an utterly off-hand manner, perhaps even with a touch of scorn and loathing. In general, she refuses to conceal the fact that I disgust her so much. I can see it very well. But despite that, she doesn't hide from me the fact that she needs me for some purpose, and that for this reason she is sparing me. A strange relationship has been established between us, which in many aspects is beyond my understanding, when I think how proud and haughty she is toward everyone else. She knows, for instance, how desperately in love with her I am. She even tolerates my speaking of my passion—and, of course, she couldn't show me more contempt than by allowing me to hold forth about my love, unhindered and uncensored. It is as if she were saying to me that she cared so little about me that it made no difference to her what I said to her or how I felt about her.

Even before, she often spoke to me about her private affairs, but never with complete frankness. There was a certain refinement in her contempt for me. It didn't bother her, for instance, to know that I was aware of some circumstance in her life, or that something was worrying her a great deal. In fact, she was prepared to reveal a secret to me if she wanted to use me as her slave or errand boy, but then she'd tell me only what an errand boy needed to know—and although I still knew nothing of the whole pattern of events, although she herself could see how much I suffered and worried about her sufferings and worries, she never bothered to reassure me by speaking to me frankly, like a friend. And since she used me on difficult and even dangerous errands, I feel she owed me a frank explanation.

Anyway, why bother about my feelings, about the fact that I can worry too, and am perhaps three times more concerned than she is herself about her cares and hurts?

I knew three weeks in advance that she intended to play roulette. She had informed me that I would have to play for her, because it was unbecoming for her to do so herself. From her tone I gathered that she had some serious preoccupation beyond the wish to win some money. What could money in itself mean to her? She was pursuing a goal, there was a secret involved at which I might try to guess, but of which I still knew nothing. Of course, the position of bondage and humiliation in which she held me could have given me—and often did give me —the opportunity to question her directly, point-blank. Indeed, since I am her slave and an utter nonentity in her eyes, she couldn't possibly take offense at my impudent curiosity. But the trouble is that, while she does tolerate my asking her questions, she doesn't bother to answer them. At times, indeed, she ignores them altogether. That is how we get along!

There was a lot of talk yesterday about a wire sent to Petersburg four days before, which had remained unanswered. The General is visibly worried. Obviously it is about the Grandmother. The Frenchman is worried, too. Yesterday, the two of them had a long and serious talk after lunch. The Frenchman's tone toward all of us is extraordinarily haughty and contemptuous. He acts just like the pig in the saying: A pig invited to the table will put its feet on it. Even with Paulina, his behavior borders on rudeness, although he seems to enjoy taking part in our walks in the Casino park and in our rides through the countryside.

I have been aware for a long time of certain circumstances that link the Frenchman with the General. At one time they were thinking of opening a factory in Russia, and I am not sure whether the plan fell through or whether they are still talking about it. And also, by chance, I found out a part of the family secret: last year, the Frenchman really pulled the General out of trouble, giving him thirty thousand rubles to make up a deficit in government monies missing on the day of the General's retirement. And so, of course, he had the General in his clutches. Nevertheless, I am quite certain that it is Mademoiselle Blanche who is playing the main role now. Yes, there's no possible doubt about that.

And who is she? Here, people say she is a distinguished Frenchwoman who lives with her mother and has a fabulous fortune. It is also known that she is a relation of our Marquis, although only a distant cousin or something of the sort. I gather that before my trip to Paris the Frenchman and Mademoiselle Blanche treated each other with refined politeness, while now their kinship manifests itself by rather more familiar, quite unceremonious relations. It may be that our position looks so desperate now that they don't feel they have to go on putting on a show for our benefit.

The day before yesterday, I noticed the way Mr. Astley was watching Mademoiselle Blanche and her mother. I got the impression that he had met both them and the Frenchman before. But with Mr. Astley being so shy, reserved, and taciturn, he can be relied on not to commit an indiscretion. At least, the Frenchman hardly acknowledged his presence, almost ignoring him; so he wasn't afraid of him. Well, that seems to make sense. But why should Mademoiselle Blanche almost ignore him, too? I was struck by the fact that when, during a general conversation, the Marquis suddenly blurted out about Mr. Astley being immensely rich, she still continued to ignore the Englishman, which was quite out of keeping with what I knew about Mademoiselle Blanche.

And so it is quite understandable that the General should worry, and one can well imagine what a telegram announcing the death of the Grandmother would mean to him.

I had the impression that Paulina was deliberately avoiding me and, although I affected a cold and indifferent air myself, I kept hoping that she would come over and talk to me.

But yesterday and today my attention has mostly been centered around Mademoiselle Blanche. The poor General, he is irredeemably lost! To fall so passionately in love when one is past fifty is a misfortune in itself; but in his case you have to add the fact that he is a widower with children, and also his complete bankruptcy, his debts, and, finally, the sort of woman he has fallen for.

Mademoiselle Blanche is beautiful. But I am not sure if I will be understood if I say that she has one of those faces that can frighten you. I, at least, have always been afraid of women of her sort. I'd say she is about twenty-five. She is tall and her shoulders are broad and attractively curved; her neck and bosom are gorgeous; she has an olive complexion, her hair is black as India ink, and there is enough of it for two hairdos. Her eyes are dark, their whites yellowish; her look is arrogant, her teeth flashing white, her lips are always reddened, and she gives off a slight smell of musk. She wears very striking and expensive clothes, but always with very good taste. Her hands and feet are lovely; her voice is a deep contralto. At times she'll burst out laughing, showing all her teeth, but mostly she maintains a haughty silence—at least in the presence of Paulina and Maria Filipovna (by the way, I've heard a strange rumor that Maria Filipovna is leaving for Russia).

I have the impression that Mademoiselle Blanche is rather uneducated and maybe not even very intelligent, although she is certainly careful and cunning. I'd venture to say that she's had many adventures in her life. Well, to tell the truth, I wouldn't be too surprised if it turned out that the Marquis was not really a relation of hers, and her alleged mother not her mother at all. On the other hand, though, there is evidence that in Berlin, where we met them, she and her mother had a few impressive connections.

As to the Marquis himself, although I am still very

doubtful about his being a genuine marquis, there can be no doubt that he has been around in high society, both in Moscow and in Berlin. I have no idea about his position in his native France. They say he owns a château there.

I had thought that in the two weeks I was away many things would have happened here, but to this day I don't know for sure whether anything definite has been said between the General and Mademoiselle Blanche. I believe that much depends on our situation, that is, on the amount of money the General will be able to flash before them. If, for instance, news had arrived that the Grandmother had recovered, I am certain that Mademoiselle Blanche would have vanished immediately. But I must say it strikes me as funny when I think what a gossip I have become. Ah, how disgusted I am with it all! With what joy would I send everything and everybody to hell! But can I really leave Paulina? Can I stop spying around her? I realize, of course, how despicable spying is, but what do I care?

Mr. Astley, too, has been behaving rather strangely, both yesterday and today. Yes, I am quite convinced that he is in love with Paulina. It is curious and very funny how much can be grasped from the expression of a shy, morbidly timid man when he is in love, especially since he would rather be swallowed up by the earth than allow himself to express his feelings by a word or a glance. We meet Mr. Astley quite often during our walks. He always takes off his hat and passes by, although he is obviously dying to join us. Even when we explicitly invite him to do so, he always declines immediately. But wherever we are—near the Casino, by the fountain, in the park, in the wood or on the Schlangenberg—we only have to look around and, sure enough, there is a bit of Mr. Astley showing from behind a bush or around the corner of a near-by path. I believe he is looking for an opportunity to have a private talk with me. This morning we met and exchanged a few words. At times, he sounds exceedingly abrupt. This time, without saying good morning, he began:

"Ah, that Mademoiselle Blanche! I've seen so many women like her."

He fell silent, giving me a meaningful look. I am not sure what he meant by it, for when I asked him, "What do you mean?" he smiled cunningly and muttered, "Just that."

Then he inquired: "Does Miss Paulina like flowers very much?"

"I have no idea," I said.

"What! You don't know?" he cried, very surprised.

"No, I don't. I haven't paid any attention to the matter," I said, laughing.

"Hm, that gives me an idea," he muttered, then bowed to me and walked off.

But I must say he looked rather pleased. We communicate, he and I, in execrable French.

IV

This has been a ridiculous, hideous, preposterous day. It is eleven in the evening. I am sitting in my room and going over it. It started in the morning when, despite everything, I went to play roulette for Paulina. I took her sixteen hundred gulden under two conditions: one, that I would not go halves with her in it, that is, I wouldn't have any share in the winnings; and two, that in the evening Paulina should explain to me why it was so important for her to win, and exactly how much money she needed. For I still couldn't believe that she was simply after money for its own sake—she obviously needed it for something special. She promised to give me an explanation, and I went to the Casino.

The gaming rooms were terribly crowded, and the crowd struck me now as unbearably ill-mannered and greedy. I elbowed my way to the table and installed myself near the croupier. I began to play very cautiously, risking only one or two coins at a time. At the same time, I looked around, noting things. I decided that calculations meant little, and certainly didn't have the importance attached to them by many gamblers. They sit there with sheets of ruled paper, note the numbers that come up, evaluate the chances, place their stakes accordingly, and proceed to lose just like us mere mortals who are gambling without a system. But despite that, I was able to draw one conclusion, which I believe to be correct: it is true that in the series of random winning numbers there is, if not a strict order, at least a certain pattern, which, of course, is very strange. For instance, it happens that when the twelve middle numbers have come up, it is the turn of the twelve last numbers; then, assuming that these last numbers come up twice, it will be the turn of the first twelve. Now, after the first twelve, it is the turn of the middle twelve again; they come up three or four times in a row, and then it is the last twelve once more and they win twice, and then the first twelve take over to win once, after which the middle twelve win three times; and it goes on thus for an hour and a half or two hours. One, three, and two; one, three, and two. It is very amusing. Some days, or sometimes just in the morning, it may so happen that the red and the black alternate back and forth, almost without pattern and changing every minute, so that neither the red nor the black ever wins more than three or four times in a row. But on another day, or in the evening, it may happen that a red will come up as many as twenty-two times in a row, and it will go on like that for some time, perhaps even for the whole day. Much of this was explained to me by Mr. Astley, who had spent a whole morning at one of the roulette tables without once playing himself.

As for me, I lost everything very quickly. I placed two hundred gulden directly on the "evens," and won. I staked them again and won again, and then again doubled my winnings two or three times more in the same way. I believe I had something like four thousand gulden in my hands within five minutes. That's when I should have quit. But a funny feeling came over me, some sort of a desire to challenge Fate, an uncontrollable urge to stick my tongue out at it, to give it a flip on the nose. So I played the maximum permissible single stake, which was four thousand gulden, and lost. Then, in my excitement, I placed all the money I had left on the same color, and lost again.

I left the table stunned, as if by a blow. I couldn't even understand what had happened, and didn't announce the disaster to Paulina until just before lunch. While waiting for the meal, I roamed aimlessly through the park.

During lunch, I was in the same excited state I had been in three days earlier. The Frenchman and Mademoiselle Blanche were again having lunch with us. It turned out that Mademoiselle Blanche had been in the gaming room that morning and had witnessed my exploits. This time she seemed to pay me a little more attention. The Frenchman was quite direct—he asked me point-blank whether it was my own money I had lost. I believe he suspected Paulina. In brief, there was something going on there. So I lied and told him that the money was mine.

The General was very surprised: where could I possibly have got the money from? I explained that I had started with one hundred gulden, that six or seven wins in a row had brought my holdings up to five or six thousand gulden, and that I had lost it after that in two goes.

Of course, it was quite credible, and as I said it I stole a glance at Paulina. But I couldn't decipher anything in her face. Still, she had allowed me to lie without setting it straight, so I concluded I had done the right thing in lying and in concealing the fact that I had been playing in her behalf. She owes me an explanation, I thought to myself, and anyway, she has promised to let me in on a few things.

I thought the General would make some comment or other, but he said nothing, although his face was tense and worried. Perhaps, pressed financially as he was, it was simply painful to him to hear of a fool like me letting such a pile of gold come and go within a quarter of an hour.

I suspect he had a heated argument with the Frenchman

last night. They locked themselves in a room and had a rather long and unpleasant conversation. The Frenchman left looking irritated, but this morning he came to see the General again, apparently to continue their talk.

When he heard my explanation, the Frenchman remarked in an insulting and even angry tone that I ought to have had more sense. Then, I don't know why, he added that although many Russians went in for gambling, in his opinion they weren't even good at that.

"And in my opinion, roulette is made to measure for Russians," I said, and when the Frenchman simply answered that with a snort of contempt, I told him that I was certainly right, because in saying that the Russians were a race of gamblers, I was rather maligning than praising them and that, therefore he could take my word for it.

"But on what do you base your opinion?" he asked.

"On the fact that, in the course of history, the ability to accumulate capital had come almost to head the list of virtues required by a man reared in Western civilization. But the Russian is not only incapable of accumulating capital, he is also a persistent and hopeless squanderer. Nonetheless, we Russians do have great use for money, and so we are always very happy to come across such things as roulette, which can enable a man to become rich effortlessly within two hours. That is very tempting to us and, since we gamble haphazardly, as we do everything else, without bothering to make the effort to think, we are bound to lose everything we have."

"There is quite a bit of truth in what you say," the Frenchman said smugly.

"No, you are being unfair, and you should be ashamed of yourself, running down your country like that," the General observed sternly.

"Yes," I said, "but even so, it still remains to be seen which is more repulsive—Russian haphazardness or German accumulation of wealth through honest labor."

"What a monstrous thought!" the General cried.

"How very Russian!" the Frenchman exclaimed.

I laughed. I wanted very much to goad them.

"For my part," I said, "I'd rather spend my life like a nomad under a tent than worship the German idol."

"What idol?" the General snapped, becoming really angry.

"The German method of accumulating wealth. I haven't been here very long, but what I have already managed to observe and check is enough to outrage my Tartar nature. I assure you, I want none of their virtues! Yesterday, I went for a six- or seven-mile walk through the town and the countryside, and it all looked to me exactly like the illustrations in those little German manuals of moral principle. Every house here has its *Vater*, a frightfully virtuous and infinitely honorable man. In fact, he is so honorable that it's frightening to come too close to him. Well, I personally can't stand people who are that honorable! And each of these *Vaters* has a family, and in the evenings they all sit together and read wholesome, edifying books. And above the housetops, elms and chestnuts rustle, a stork nests on the roof, and the sun sets behind it, and everything is so supremely poetic and touching.

"Please, don't be angry, General, and allow me to tell you something that is really most moving. I remember evenings when my late father also sat under the lime trees, reading that sort of book aloud to my mother and me. So I am quite qualified to speak of it. And so, each family around here owes slavish obedience to its *Vater*. They must all work like beasts of burden and amass money like Jewish usurers. Now let's suppose the *Vater* has amassed a sum of money and is reckoning on his oldest son to take over his trade and possessions. So he gives no dowry to his daughter and she stays an old maid all her life. Then he sells his younger sons into bondage or to the army, and the proceeds go to swell the family capital. Believe me, that is the way it is done here. I have inquired. And it is all done for honorable reasons, for reasons so ultra-honorable that even the youngest son, who has been sold,

43

is convinced that it was done out of supremely honorable motives—and this certainly is an ideal situation, when the victim himself is delighted to be led to the altar.

"Well, and what next? The next point is that it doesn't make the oldest son any better off. His heart may be longing for some Gretchen, but he cannot be lawfully united with her because he still hasn't accumulated a sufficient amount of cash. And so they wait virtuously, accepting the sacrifice with a smile. In the meantime, Gretchen's cheeks grow hollow, she withers. . . . At last, perhaps twenty years later, it is decided that their prosperity has been sufficiently increased, that enough cash has been honestly earned and virtuously saved. The *Vater* blesses his forty-year-old heir and his thirty-five-year-old betrothed, whose bosom is now sunken and whose nose has turned red. . . . And with that, the *Vater* weeps and moralizes, and finally dies.

"And the oldest son becomes a virtuous *Vater* in his turn and the story is repeated.

"Then, in fifty or maybe seventy years, the grandson of the first *Vater* at last has a really substantial amount of capital to turn over to his son, who turns it over to his, and so on, for five or six generations, when the descendants may be a Baron Rothschild, or Hoppe and Co., the Amsterdam bankers, or God knows who. Well, gentlemen, isn't it a really awe-inspiring sight? The centuries-long effort, the hard work in relays, the patience, the character, the determination, the thrift, the stork on the roof! What else could one wish for? There certainly is nothing loftier. And so, these people begin to judge the rest of the world by their own standards and condemn those who diverge from them, that is, those who are different.

"Well, that is how it is, and I for my part definitely prefer to let myself go, Russian fashion, or to try to become rich quickly by playing roulette. I have no wish whatever to turn into Hoppe and Co. in five generations. I need money for my personal use and refuse to consider

myself as an instrument for the accumulation of capital.
. . . All right, I know I have said many inane things, but
I stand by them. These are my convictions."

"I don't know how much truth there is in what you've
said," the General said musingly, "but of one thing I am
sure: whenever you're given half a chance, you become in-
sufferably overbearing, and . . ."

As usual, he didn't finish his thought. Whenever he
touched upon a subject that went a bit deeper than the
ordinary conversation, he always left his sentences un-
finished.

The Frenchman had listened open-eyed but with affected
nonchalance. Paulina looked haughty and bored. She didn't
seem to have taken in a word of the conversation.

V

She seemed immersed in her thoughts, but as soon as
we got up from the table she said she was going to take
the children out for a walk and asked me to come with
her. We all went off toward the fountain.

In my agitated state, I asked her with stupid offensive-
ness why it was that her Des Grieux—the little Frenchie
—never accompanied her on her strolls any more, and why,
indeed, he had lately sometimes hardly even addressed her
for days on end.

"Because he is a beast," she said in a strange voice.

I had never heard her say such a thing about him before, and I fell silent, afraid to try to understand what
her exasperation might imply.

"And did you notice," I said after a while, "that things
were very tense between him and the General today?"

"Wouldn't you like to know what it's all about?" she
said, with cold irritation. "You know very well that the
General has mortgaged everything to him, that the whole

estate belongs to him, and that if Grandmother isn't dead, the Frenchman will immediately enter into possession of everything that has been pledged to him."

"So it's really true that everything has been mortgaged? I'd heard that, but I never realized that it was actually everything."

"Well, now you know."

"But then, it's good-bye to Mademoiselle Blanche—she'll never marry the General. And you know what?" I went on. "The General seems to have fallen for her so strongly that he is quite likely to shoot himself if she jilts him. It is dangerous to fall in love like that at his age."

"I too feel that something awful will happen to him," Paulina said abstractedly.

"How beautiful!" I said. "It would be quite impossible to demonstrate more clearly that she consented to do it just for the money's sake. They haven't even bothered to save appearances—it is all quite open. It's really wonderful! As to the Grandmother, what could be more ridiculous and, for that matter, more disgusting, than to keep sending telegram after telegram asking, 'Is she dead?' 'Has she died at last?' Well, what do you say, Paulina, don't you think it's great?"

"Nonsense!" she said with distaste. "What surprises me at the moment is that you should be so cheerful just now. What are you so pleased about? Is it because you lost all my money?"

"Why did you give it to me to lose? Didn't I tell you I couldn't play for others, and least of all for you? I do whatever you tell me, but the results don't depend on me. Why, I warned you that no good would come of it. Tell me, are you very desperate at having lost all that money? I wish I knew what you need so much for."

"Why do you ask all these questions?"

"But, remember, you promised to explain to me. . . . Listen, I am quite convinced that when I start playing for myself—and I possess a hundred and twenty gulden—I'll win. Well, then you'll take whatever you need out of my money."

46

Her expression became disdainful.

"Please don't be angry at my offer," I went on. "I feel so deeply that I don't count as far as you are concerned, that I am nothing in your eyes, that you can really accept anything from me, even money. You cannot feel degraded in accepting money from me, especially since I've lost yours."

She gave me a quick glance and, obviously realizing that I was irritated and was being sarcastic, changed the conversation once again.

"There is nothing so very intriguing in my situation. But if you must know, I simply owe that money. I borrowed it, and would like to pay it back. I had a strange and crazy notion—I felt sure I would win at roulette here. Why I thought so, I can't explain, but I felt sure of it. Who knows, perhaps I believed it only because I had no alternative left."

"It's because you simply *had to* win. It is like a drowning man grasping at a straw. You must realize yourself that if he weren't drowning, he couldn't possibly mistake the straw for a floating branch."

Paulina was surprised. "Why, but you too are clinging to a straw! A couple of weeks ago, you explained to me at great length that you were absolutely sure to win at roulette, and then you rushed away because I stared at you as if you were insane. Or perhaps you were joking then? No, I remember very clearly that you were absolutely serious, and it didn't sound like a joke at all."

"That's true," I said dreamily. "Even now, I am still convinced I'll win. And let me confess to you that you have led me to ask myself: why is it that even my shocking and idiotic loss today hasn't raised any misgivings in my mind. I still feel just as convinced as ever that as soon as I start playing on my own account I can't fail to win."

"But what makes you so sure?"

"Well, since you press me—I don't know. All I can tell you is that I *must* win, that it is the only way out for me. Well, maybe that's why I feel so sure."

"Then I suppose you too absolutely *must* win, if you are so fanatically convinced?"

"I bet you doubt that I am able to feel the absolute necessity of anything."

"Well, I don't really care," Paulina said in a quiet, tired voice, "although I must say I do doubt that you could be seriously tormented by anything. You could be tormented, yes, but not seriously. You are too irresponsible and vague for that. What do you need money for? In all the explanations you offered me that time, I couldn't find one serious reason—"

"By the way," I said, interrupting her, "you told me you had to pay back a debt. Would you owe money to the Frenchman, by any chance?"

"Why all these questions? You're so rude today! Are you drunk, by any chance?"

"You know I allow myself to speak my mind, and at times I feel entitled to ask very frank questions. I repeat, I am your slave, and a master cannot be ashamed before a slave or offended by him."

"All that's sheer, stupid nonsense. I can't stand that 'slave theory' of yours."

"Please note, though, that I don't say I am your slave because that's what I want to be. I am simply stating a fact that is quite independent of my wishes."

"Now give me a straightforward answer: why do you need money?"

"Why do you want to know?"

"Please yourself," she said, proudly tossing her head.

"I see that while you hate my 'slave theory' you still demand that I behave like your slave: 'Just answer and don't argue'—that sort of thing. All right, then, you want to know why I need money? Well, money is everything, that's why."

"I understand, but why should you want it to the point of going insane? Why, you seem to get into a state of exaltation about it and plunge into mysticism. You must have some special reason to want money that much. I want a straightforward answer."

She seemed to be really losing her temper, and I loved her angry questioning.

"Of course I have a reason for wanting money," I said. "But I can't very well explain it beyond saying that if I had money I'd become a man in your eyes instead of a slave."

"And how do you propose to achieve that?"

"How will I achieve it? Is it possible that you can't even imagine yourself regarding me as anything but a slave? Well, I no longer want you to feel like that."

"But didn't you claim yourself that this slavery is a joy to you? Well, I must say I thought so myself."

"You thought so yourself!" I repeated with a strange feeling of pleasure. "What a delightfully innocent admission, coming from you! Well, yes, it's true—being your slave is a joy to me, for there is joy in the last degree of abasement and humiliation," I went on deliriously. "And who knows, maybe there is pleasure under the whip too when it lashes your back and tears your flesh to pieces. . . . But it's possible that I feel like trying some other kinds of joy now. Yesterday the General lectured me at the dinner table, feeling entitled to do so because he pays me seven hundred rubles a year, which I am not so sure he'll be able to pay. And the Marquis des Grieux looks at me with raised eyebrows and, at the same time, doesn't notice me. And what if I, for my part, am passionately longing to catch the Marquis by the nose right in front of you?"

"That's a lot of immature nonsense! Whatever the situation, it is always possible to behave with dignity. A clash of wills doesn't degrade, it elevates."

"That sounds as if it came straight out of a good-behavior manual! Maybe you imagine I don't know how to behave with dignity. That is, I may be a person worthy of respect, but one quite incapable of commanding it from others. You do understand, then, that that can happen? Yes, and all Russians are like that, because Russians are too richly endowed and too versatile to find an appropriate way to behave right away. It's all a matter of form. We Russians are so richly endowed by nature that it takes genius to find an appropriate code of behavior. But usually we fall short of genius, because it is a rare thing anyway. It is only among the French, and perhaps among a few other European nations, that the proper form has become so clearly defined that it is quite possible to behave with dignity while being an utterly despicable person. And that's why they attach such importance to external form. A Frenchman will put up with a real, profound insult without wincing, but he won't stand having his nose flipped, because it is a breach of the accepted and time-honored code of behavior. And that's why our young ladies fall for the French so easily—they have such good form. But in my personal opinion, there is no good form in it whatever, nothing but *le coq gaulois*. But probably I simply cannot understand, not being a woman. Perhaps the Gallic roosters really are great.

"But I believe I'm talking nonsense now. Why don't you stop me? You know, you ought to stop me more often when I talk to you, because I want to tell you everything, everything. I lose all sense of form. I agree that I not only don't possess good form, but I lack all the virtues too. I advise you of that fact. And I am not even worried about dignity either. Everything inside me has come to a stop now. And you know very well why. There is not a single scrap of human thought in my head. I lost touch with what's going on in the world, in Russia, around here, a long time ago. . . . Recently, for instance, I went through Dresden, but I couldn't tell you what sort of a place Dresden is. You know yourself what has swallowed me up. And since there is no hope for me and I am nothing in your eyes, I can tell you openly: I see only you everywhere I go, and I don't care a thing for the rest. I don't know why or how I love you. Let me tell you—it is quite possible that you aren't even beautiful. Can you imagine, I don't even know whether your face is pretty or not. Your heart is certainly not good, and I doubt that you have a noble soul."

"So that's what makes you think you can buy me with money—because I haven't a noble soul."

"Whenever did I want to buy you with money?" I protested.

"You're getting all mixed up and forgetting your own arguments. And even if it wasn't actually me you wanted to buy with money, you imagined that money could pay for my respect."

"No, it's not quite like that. I warned you it would be hard for me to make you understand. You make me feel small. Please forgive my drivel. Try to understand that you shouldn't really be angry with me—I am simply insane. But after all, if you wish to, go ahead and be angry—it's all the same to me. When I am all alone upstairs in my attic room, all I have to do is to imagine the rustle of your dress and I can bite my hands till they bleed. And why are you angry with me? Because I call myself your slave? Well, please, please, go on taking advantage of my bondage! Do you know that one day I'll end up killing you? And it won't be out of jealousy or because I've stopped loving you, but simply because there are moments when I long to eat you. You're laughing. . . ."

"I'm not laughing at all," she said irately. "I demand that you keep still."

She stopped, quite out of breath from sheer indignation. I swear I couldn't say whether she was beautiful or not, but I always loved to watch her glaring angrily at me like that, and that's why I like to provoke her. Perhaps she had noticed it and had lost her temper on purpose. I wondered about that out loud.

"Disgusting!" she cried.

"I don't care," I said. "And let me tell you—it is quite dangerous for us to walk out alone: several times I've had a vague notion to beat you up, to maim you, to strangle you. And why shouldn't it come to that? You are driving me to a frenzy. You certainly don't imagine that I would be afraid of a scandal, or of displeasing you? What do I care about your anger? I love you without hope, and I know that after I'd done it my love would even be a thousand times stronger. And if I do kill you one day, you must realize that I'll have to kill myself too. Well, then,

I'll go as long as possible without killing myself in order to savor the unbearable torture of living without you. It is really incredible, but every day I love you more and more, which seems quite impossible. And in view of that, how can I help being a fatalist?

"Do you remember, two days ago, on the Schlangenberg, when you called me to your side, I whispered to you: 'Say the word and I will jump.' If you'd said the word, I'd have jumped. Do you really not believe me?"

"Such stupid nonsense!"

"I don't care whether what I say is stupid or not," I said. "All I know is that when I'm with you I must talk and talk and talk, and so I talk. I lose all my self-respect when I am with you, and I don't care."

"Why on earth should I demand that you jump from the Schlangenberg?" she said coldly and somehow especially insultingly. "That would be quite useless to me."

"Magnificent!" I cried. "You said that word 'useless' so deliberately and so beautifully, just to crush me. I see through you so well! So it would be useless, you say? But isn't pleasure always useful? And isn't savage, unlimited power, be it only over a fly, also a sort of voluptuous joy? A human being is a natural despot and likes to inflict pain. You love it terribly."

I remember her looking at me with a strange intentness. Possibly my face at that moment expressed all my absurd and incoherent feelings. I remember now that our conversation was almost word for word as I have just given it. My eyes were bloodshot. There was foam at the corners of my mouth. As to the Schlangenberg, I swear on my honor that if she had told me to jump from it I'd have jumped. Even if she'd said it as a joke, even if she'd spat at me with scorn while telling me to leap, I'd have obeyed.

"Why, I do believe you," she said, pronouncing the words as she alone could pronounce them, putting so much sneering scorn, contempt, and disgust into them that, by God, I could have killed her then and there. She was taking a risk. I'd warned her about that.

"You're not a coward, are you?" she asked suddenly.

"I don't know. Maybe I am a coward. I haven't given it a thought for a long time."

"If I told you: 'Kill this man,' would you do it?"

"Whom?"

"Whomever I might choose."

"The Frenchman?"

"Don't question me, just answer—would you kill anyone I pointed out to you? I want to know whether you meant all the things you were saying just now."

She was waiting so intently and so impatiently for me to answer that it made me feel very strange.

"Well, are you going to tell me finally what this is all about?" I shouted. "Why, are you afraid of me, or what? I can see the whole shabby set-up for myself! You're the stepdaughter of a ruined and crazy man who had been contaminated by a passion for that hellcat Blanche. Then, there is that Frenchman who has some mysterious power over you. . . . And here you are, asking me a question like that. Whatever else, I must know what's going on, for otherwise I'm likely to go mad and do something. Unless you're ashamed to tell me the truth? But how can you be ashamed before me?"

"We weren't talking about all that just now—I simply asked you a question, and am waiting for your reply."

"Of course I'll kill for you!" I cried. "I'll kill anyone you tell me to, but will you really ask me to do that?"

"Why, what do you imagine—that I'll abstain out of consideration for you? I'll tell you to do it and remain in the background myself. Will you be able to stand that? No, I don't suppose you're made of such stuff! If you killed a man on my orders, you'd come back to kill me too afterward, because I dared to make you do it."

It felt like a blow on the head when she said those words. And although, even then, I thought she wasn't really serious, that she was just daring me, there was too much seriousness in the tone in which she had said it. What struck me was that she had put it the way she had, that she reserved to herself such a right over me, that she accepted her power over me, saying in effect, "You'll go to your death and I'll remain safely behind." There was such frank cynicism in her attitude that I felt it was too much even for me. Well, in that case, what was I really in her eyes? This was something that went beyond the bounds of slavery and degradation. After such a way of looking at a man, she was bound to raise him to her own level. Incredible as our conversation was, my heart felt faint.

Suddenly she burst out laughing. At that moment, we were sitting on a bench in front of where the children were playing and facing the spot where the carriages stopped to unload their passengers at the entrance to the path leading to the Casino.

"Do you see that fat woman?" she said, still laughing. "She's the Baroness Wurmerhelm. She's been here only three days. Do you see that tall, thin Prussian with a cane? That's her husband. Do you remember how he looked at us day before yesterday? I want you to go over to the Baroness now, take off your hat, and say something to her in French."

"Why should I?"

"You've just been swearing that you would jump from the Schlangenberg if I demanded it of you. Well, instead of murders and tragedies, I simply want to have a good laugh. Go on, and don't argue. I'll enjoy watching the Baron swing at you with his cane."

"Are you daring me? You think I won't do it?"

"Yes, I am daring you. Go on, I want you to."

"All right, I'll go, although it's really a stupid whim. I only hope there won't be any unpleasant consequences for the General, and then, through him, for you. I assure you, I'm not worried for myself, but for you and perhaps for the General. And what a strange idea—to insult a woman?"

"Well, I see now that you're nothing but a windbag," she said scornfully. "It was just that your eyes were bloodshot a moment ago, and even that was perhaps because you had too much wine to drink at lunch. Don't you think I can see for myself that what I am asking you to do is both stupid and vulgar, and that the General is bound to be angry? But I want to have a laugh. Well, I want it, and that's all there is to it. And you won't even have to insult the lady. They'll give you your thrashing before that."

I turned away and silently went to do what she'd asked me to. It was all quite absurd, and I, of course, should have managed to get out of it somehow. But as I drew closer to the Baroness I began to feel like playing a prank myself. Yes, I felt very much like playing a schoolboy prank then and there. I was terribly excited and felt rather as if I were drunk.

VI

Now two days have passed since that idiotic incident. What a lot of noise, shouting, and fuss there was, what a display of vulgarity, bad manners, and stupidity! And I was the cause of it all. But in retrospect it seems rather funny. To me, at least. I cannot explain what has come over me, whether I am really in an exalted state or whether I've just slipped out of my mind and will go on perpetrating outrages until they lock me up. There are moments when I have the impression that my mind is quite clouded, and at others I feel as though I were just out of school and still enjoy playing schoolboy pranks.

It was all Paulina's fault, of course! Probably I wouldn't have behaved so childishly if it hadn't been for her. And who knows, I may be doing all this out of despair (however stupid such reasoning may sound). And I can't really see what's so good about her. Well, no, she's beautiful all right; at least I believe she is. Why, other people are crazy about her, too. She's tall and slender. Though too slender perhaps. I feel as if I could take her and tie her in a knot or fold her in two. Her foot is long, narrow, and tantalizing. Yes, exactly that—tantalizing. There is a reddish light in her hair and her eyes are just like a cat's, but then, she can look out of them with such regal pride. One evening about four months ago, only a few days after I had joined them, she was having a heated talk with Des Grieux in the drawing room. And she looked at him in such a way that when I got back to my room to go to bed, I imagined she had slapped him; that she had just slapped him and was now standing in front of him and looking at him. . . . And that was when I fell in love with her.

But let's get back to business.

I stepped onto the path, planted myself in the middle of it, and waited for the Baron and the Baroness. When they were five paces away, I took off my hat and bowed.

I remember the Baroness was wearing a dress of light gray silk with a rather unencompassable waistline, with flounces, crinoline, and train. She was quite short, extraordinarily fat, with a huge, hanging, multiple chin that completely hid her neck. Her face was purplish, her eyes wicked and arrogant, and her way of walking suggested that she was conferring a great honor upon all those in sight.

The Baron was lean and lanky. His face, like so many German faces, was asymmetrical and crisscrossed by a multitude of tiny wrinkles. He was about forty-five, and wore spectacles. His legs started almost at his chest—there's breeding for you!—and he strutted along like a peacock. The expression of his face somehow made one think of a ram, and that is a good substitute for wisdom.

My eye took all this in within three seconds.

At first they hardly noticed my bow and the fact that I was holding my hat in my hand. The Baron just scowled a little and the Baroness came on at full sail toward me.

"*Madame la baronne,*" I said pronouncing each word with the greatest clarity, "*j'ai l'honneur d'être votre esclave!*"

I bowed again, put on my hat, and walked off, passing very close to the Baron and looking at him all the while with a smile.

It was Paulina who had ordered me to take off my hat,

but the bows and the monkeyshines were my voluntary contributions. God knows what prompted me to do it. I felt as though I were falling from the top of a cliff. . . .

"What's that?" the Baron shouted, or more accurately, screeched, turning toward me in angry surprise.

I faced him and stood in respectful expectation, still looking into his face and smiling. His brows contracted to the utmost. His face grew darker and darker. The Baroness was also facing me now, and she too was glaring at me in outraged surprise. People were looking at us; some even stopped and stared.

"What's that?" the Baron shouted again, screeching twice as loudly in redoubled anger.

"*Ja wohl!*" I drawled, my eyes still fixed on his.

"*Sind sie rasend?*" he screamed, waving his stick.

I believe he was feeling a bit nervous. Possibly it was my costume that took him aback. I was dressed quite well, even elegantly, and looked as if I belonged to the best society.

"*Ja wo-o-ohl!*" I suddenly cried at the top of my voice, drawing out the letter *o* like the Berliners, who often use the phrase, and drawl the letter *o* in different ways to express various nuances of mood and feeling.

The Baron and the Baroness quickly turned away and all but fled from me in terror. Among the onlookers, some spoke up, others stared at me in bewilderment. But I really don't remember too well.

Unhurriedly I started walking away toward Paulina. But when I was still a hundred feet or so from her bench, she got up, took the children, and walked with them toward the hotel.

I caught up with them at the entrance.

"I have done your little bit of clowning," I said when I was close to her.

"So what?" she said, without even looking at me. "Now you'll just have to take what's coming to you." And she went upstairs.

I spent all that evening walking. I walked through the park, then passed through a wood, and even crossed the

57

boundary of the principality. I ate an omelet and drank some wine in a peasant house, for which luxury they soaked me one and a half thalers.

It was eleven when I got back, and I was told at once that the General wanted to see me immediately.

Our party occupied two suites in the hotel—four rooms altogether. The first and largest was the drawing room, with a piano in it. Next to it was another large room, which the General had made into his study. It was here that he was waiting for me, standing in the middle of the room in a rather majestic pose. Des Grieux was sitting on the couch nearby him.

"May I inquire, young man, what it is you've done?" the General began, looking at me.

"I would appreciate it, General, if you would come straight to the point," I said, "for I assume that you wish to talk to me about the encounter I had today with a certain German."

"A certain German, indeed! That German happens to be a very important one—he is Baron Wurmerhelm! And you were rude to the Baroness."

"I wasn't."

"You frightened them, sir!" the General said, raising his voice.

"Oh no, I certainly didn't do that! The thing is, when I was in Berlin I became fascinated by the phrase *ja wohl,* which the Germans use every minute, and which they drag out rather repulsively. Well then, when I met that man on the path, the phrase *ja wohl* suddenly came into my mind and had an irritating effect upon me. . . . And on top of that, the Baroness was walking straight at me according to her habit—she had done it three times before when we met in the street—as if I were a worm she could squash underfoot. I suppose you'll agree that I too have a right to my dignity. So I removed my hat, very politely, I assure you, and said: *'Madame, je suis votre esclave.'* And when the Baron stared at me and said, 'What's that?' I couldn't help shouting back, *'Ja wohl.'* I shouted it exactly twice—once pronouncing it in the usual manner, and

the second time drawing it out as much as I could. And
that's all."

I confess, I was awfully pleased with that schoolboyish
explanation. I was strangely anxious to present the story in
as absurd a light as possible.

And the further I went, the more I enjoyed it.

"You seem to be making fun of me!" the General
snapped. Then he turned toward the Frenchman and told
him in French that I was obviously looking for trouble.
Des Grieux smiled scornfully and shrugged.

"Please, you mustn't think that, General!" I said plead-
ingly. "Although, of course, I confess it wasn't the right
thing to do. But then, you can, at the most, describe it as
silly schoolboy stuff, nothing worse than that. And let me
tell you, sir—I am awfully sorry about my behavior now.
But I believe I have an excuse that almost releases me from
all responsibility. The thing is, I haven't been too well
these past two or three weeks. I've been feeling sick,
nervous, irritable, almost delirious, and on occasions quite
incapable of controlling myself. For instance, several times
I've felt a great longing to walk up to the Marquis des
Grieux and . . . But why go into that, after all? He may
resent it. What I mean to say is that these are the symptoms of a sickness. I am not sure, though, whether Baroness
Wurmerhelm will take my condition into consideration
when I apologize to her—I do intend to apologize. I
would be inclined to think she won't, because, as far as I
know, that excuse has recently been abused legally—at
criminal trials the defense counsels often get their clients
off by claiming that they can't remember what actually
happened at the time the crime was committed, and that
they were afflicted with a sort of sickness at that moment.
'He killed, but he can't remember a thing,' they maintain.
And, imagine, General—medical science supports them. It
is true, it confirms, that that form of sickness exists, a
temporary aberration during which a man remembers nothing, or remembers only half or only a quarter. . . . But the
Baron and the Baroness are members of the older genera-
tion and, on top of that, *junkers* and Prussian landowners,

and probably haven't yet heard of this latest development in the legal-medical world. And that's why I don't suppose they'll accept my explanation. Don't you agree, General?"

"That'll do, man!" the General said, cutting me off with suppressed anger. "I'm going to rid myself once and for all of you and your childish pranks. You won't apologize to the Baron and the Baroness, because all contact with you, be it only your apologizing, would be degrading for them. When the Baron found out that you belonged to my household, he had it out with me at the Casino, and I admit that he was not too far from demanding satisfaction of me. Now do you understand what sort of thing you've exposed me to, young man? Well, I was forced to apologize to the Baron, and I gave him my word that from that moment on you would no longer be a part of my household."

"Just a minute, just a minute, General. So it was he himself who demanded that I should no longer be part of your household, as you are pleased to put it?"

"No, he didn't—it was I who felt I had to give him that assurance, and the Baron was quite satisfied with it. We are severing our relations, sir. You have forty gulden and three florins coming to you. Here is the money and here is the accounting, so that you can check it. Good-bye. From now on, we are strangers. I've had nothing but trouble and unpleasantness from you. I'll call the manager now and warn him that, starting tomorrow, I am no longer responsible for your expenses in the hotel. And now, let me thank you for having given me the pleasure of your company, and farewell."

I took the money and the piece of paper on which my account was written, bowed to the General, and said with the utmost seriousness:

"But it can't end like this, General. I am very sorry that you have had to bear some unpleasantness from the Baron, but, if you'll excuse my saying so, it was your own fault. Why did you have to answer to the Baron for something I had done? And what does the expression that I 'belong to your household' mean? I am just a tutor in your employ, and nothing more. I am not your son and you are not my legal guardian and you cannot be responsible for my acts. I am a legally responsible person. I am twenty-five, a university graduate, and a gentleman. You and I are complete strangers. It is only my boundless respect for you that restrains me from immediately demanding satisfaction from you for having taken upon yourself the right to answer for me."

The General was so shocked that he just threw up his arms. Then he suddenly turned to the Frenchman and hurriedly explained to him in French that I had all but challenged him to a duel. The Frenchman laughed very loudly.

"But I have no intention whatever of letting the Baron off," I went on with the utmost composure, quite unabashed by Des Grieux's guffaws. "And inasmuch as you, General, in consenting to listen to the Baron's complaints and to defend his interests, have accepted a part in this affair, I have the honor to inform you that no later than tomorrow morning, I shall ask, in my own name, for a formal explanation from the Baron of why he by-passed me and addressed himself to another person about something that concerned only him and me, thus implying that I wasn't worthy to answer to him for my own acts."

What happened then was exactly what I had expected. When he heard this new piece of idiocy, the General became really scared.

"What! You intend to carry on with this damned nonsense, then! But don't you realize what it will do to me? Don't you dare, don't you dare, sir, or I swear . . . Remember, there are authorities here, too, and I will . . . Well, I could in my position . . . And the Baron could, too . . . Well, you understand, they'll lock you up. . . . The police will throw you out and prevent you from making trouble. I hope you've thought about all this. . . ."

And although he was fairly gasping with fury, I'm sure he was terribly frightened.

"General," I replied in a calm tone that was obviously unbearable to him, "they can't lock me up for anything before I have done it. I haven't demanded an explanation from the Baron yet, and you have no idea in what form and on what grounds I'll proceed. I wish only to clear up a misapprehension that is insulting to me, namely, that I am under the tutelage of someone who has power over my choice of action. There is nothing for you to worry so much about."

"For heaven's sake, for heaven's sake, Alexei, give up this crazy scheme of yours," the General muttered. He had suddenly switched from his truculent tone to a beseeching one, and even took hold of my hand. "Just think what would come of it! There'll only be more trouble. You must agree that I have to behave as discreetly as possible here, particularly at this moment. Ah, you have no idea what a delicate situation I am in! As soon as we move out of here, I am prepared to take you back. But now, I had to . . . It was just for form's sake . . . Well, I'm sure you understand, Alexei. Ah, Alexei!" he cried in despair.

Backing toward the door, I asked him once more not to worry, and promised him that I'd handle everything with care and discretion. Then I walked out hurriedly.

There are times when Russians abroad become excessively nervous, very much afraid of what people will say and think about them, and very worried over whether this or that thing is done or not. It is as if they wore a stiff corset all the time, and this is especially true of those who have some claim to prominence. They always prefer to stick slavishly to some accepted pattern of behavior in hotels, at conferences, and at places of entertainment, during their travels. But the General had just blurted out that in his case there were also some special circumstances and he had to behave with special discretion. And that was why he had suddenly become so frightened and had so abjectly changed his tone with me. I noted that. But, of course, in his panic he could still very well rush off to the authorities tomorrow, and that made it necessary for me to be careful.

Actually I had no particular wish to torment the General. What I wanted was to provoke Paulina's anger. She had been so cruel to me, forcing me into this stupid business, that now I wanted to drive her to the point where she herself would come to me and beg me to stop. My fooling might end up by compromising her too. Besides, some other feelings were taking shape in me. Even if I was willing to debase myself before her, it didn't follow that I was a wet chicken before the rest of the world, and I certainly wasn't going to allow the Baron to raise his stick to me. I felt a great desire to have a good laugh at their expense and emerge as the winner in the end. Let them watch out! I was sure she'd be afraid of a scandal and would come to me again. And if she didn't, well, she'd realize that I wasn't a wet chicken.

(I have just heard an extraordinary piece of news. I met our nurse in the hotel lobby and she told me that Maria Filipovna has taken the evening train for Karlsbad all by herself, and gone to stay with a first cousin of hers. The nurse said that she had intended to go there for a long time; but how is it, then, that no one ever heard about it before? Although, it is possible that I was the only one who didn't know. The nurse blurted out that the day before yesterday Maria Filipovna had had a heated conversation with the General. I see. It must have been about Mademoiselle Blanche. Yes, some crucial crisis is approaching.)

VII

Next morning I rang for the attendant and told him that hereafter I wanted my bill made out separately and presented to me personally. My room was not very expensive and I didn't have to leave the hotel in a rush. I had a hundred and sixty gulden, and after that . . . Well, who knows, maybe after that it would be the big money! It's a strange thing—I haven't won yet, but I am already acting, feeling, and thinking like a rich man, and I cannot conceive of myself as anything different.

Despite the early hour, I was on the point of going over to the nearby Hotel d'Angleterre to see Mr. Astley, when Des Grieux suddenly appeared. That had never happened before and, besides, that gentleman and I had been on a rather distant and unpleasant footing lately. He had been treating me with emphatic scorn and, for my part, I had no reason to like him. Indeed, I loathed him. And so I was extremely surprised at his coming to see me. I gathered that something special was brewing.

He was very amiable, and complimented me on my room. Seeing that I was holding my hat in my hand, he inquired whether I was going out for a walk at that early hour; and when I told him I was going to see Mr. Astley on business, he began to look rather worried.

Des Grieux was like all Frenchmen—he was gay and amiable when he had to be, and unbearably gloomy and dull when he felt that the effort wasn't needed. A Frenchman is seldom spontaneously friendly; his amiability is always contrived, always made to order, dictated by other considerations. And if, for instance, he thinks he ought to make a show of originality, to make a display of his fertile imagination, he prepares himself in advance; but even so, his imaginative sallies are certain to consist of the most banal, contrived, and stupid platitudes which everyone is already tired of. In his natural state, the Frenchman is the epitome of lower-middle-class practicality—in short, he is the most insufferable bore in the world. In my opinion, only those who don't know them, in particular some young Russian damsels, are fascinated by the French, whereas any self-respecting person is bound to see through and find unbearable their conventional, fixed, and stultified forms of drawing-room amiability, playfulness, and ease of manner.

"I've come to see you on business," he said very casually, although perfectly politely, "and I may as well tell you that I've come here as a representative of the General, or let's say as a mediator. Since my Russian is rather weak, I understood hardly anything of what was said yesterday, but when the General explained what it was all about, I must confess—"

"Just a minute, just a minute, Monsieur des Grieux!" I interrupted. "So you have taken it upon yourself to act as mediator in this affair. Of course, being just a humble tutor, I have never made any claim to being a close friend of the family, or anyone's confidant, and so I have no idea of what is going on. But tell me, am I to understand, then, that you now consider yourself one of the family? For otherwise, why would you get mixed up in the business and insist on acting as an intermediary on behalf of the General?"

He didn't like my question. It was too transparent for his taste, and he didn't want to tell me more than he had to.

"I am linked to the General partly by certain business interests and partly by some other considerations," he said coldly. "The General has asked me to ask you to give up the plans of which you told him last night. They are, of course, very cleverly thought out, but he asked me to make it clear to you that they won't work. The Baron won't receive you in the first place, and, then, he has at his disposal the means of preventing you from molesting him in the future. So you yourself must agree that there is not much point in your going on with it, especially as the General promises firmly to take you back into his household as soon as circumstances permit, and until then will go on paying *vos appointements*. It is rather a good arrangement for you, isn't it?"

I told him that he might be slightly wrong, that it might be that they wouldn't drive me away from the Baron's, but that perhaps, on the contrary, the Baron would hear me out; and that probably Des Grieux had really come to find out from me how I would set about the matter.

"But, my God! Since the General is so interested in this affair, it stands to reason that he would like to know how you intend to go about it—that's only natural!"

65

I started explaining to him and he listened, sprawled in an armchair, his head bent slightly sideways and an openly sarcastic expression on his face. In general, his behavior was extremely arrogant now. I pretended as hard as I could that I viewed the affair most seriously. I explained to him that since the Baron had taken it upon himself to complain against me to the General, as though I were a servant of the General, he had, in the first place, made me lose my position, and in the second place, he had treated me like a man who is not responsible for his acts and with whom it is a waste of time to speak. Obviously, I rightfully felt offended. But then, appreciating the difference in our ages and social position and so on (I could hardly keep myself from bursting out laughing at this point), I didn't wish to act irresponsibly once more by demanding satisfaction from the Baron, or even offering him satisfaction. Nevertheless, I did consider it my right to apologize to him and to the Baroness, especially since I hadn't been feeling well lately, was rather tired, and was subject to all sorts of delusions, and so on. Now, however, the Baron had put me in a position in which I could no longer apologize to him and the Baroness, since he had slighted me by going to the General over my head and by demanding that he should dismiss me, because if I did apologize everyone would think I was doing so out of fear and in order to get my position back. Hence, I must now demand that the Baron apologize to me first. Oh, I would be content with a very moderate apology, such as, for instance, his declaring that he had never intended to offend me. Well, once the Baron had said that, I'd be free to go to him and apologize frankly and with an open heart for my action. "To put it briefly," I concluded, "I am simply asking the Baron to untie my hands."

"Ah, how sensitive and refined you are! And why should you bother to apologize? But admit, Monsieur . . . Monsieur . . . that you're doing all this deliberately, just to annoy the General. Unless you have some special objective in view, *mon cher monsieur . . . pardon, j'ai oublié votre nom. . . .* It is *Monsieur Alexis, n'est ce pas?*"

"But tell me, *mon cher marquis,* what business is it of yours?"

"*Mais, le général . . .*"

"And what business is it of his? Yesterday he was telling me something about having to keep up certain standards of behavior . . . and he seemed so awfully worried. . . . But I could make neither head nor tail of it."

"There is a special circumstance involved here," Des Grieux said in a pleading tone, through which his irritation could be heard more and more distinctly. "You know Mademoiselle de Cominges, don't you?"

"You mean Mademoiselle Blanche?"

"Well, yes, of course, Blanche de Cominges . . . *et madame sa mère.* . . . You may have noticed yourself . . . Well, to make it short, the General is in love with her and it is quite possible that he will marry her right here. And imagine what would happen if there were all sorts of gossip going around and the General got involved in a scandal. . . ."

"I can't see how any gossip or scandal involving me could stop the General from marrying the lady."

"But *le baron est si irascible,* he has a typical Prussian character, *vous savez, enfin il fera une querelle d'Allemand.*"

"But it's with me that he'll quarrel, not with you people, since I no longer belong to the family," I said, trying deliberately to sound as confused as I could. "But wait, is it decided then that Mademoiselle Blanche is to marry the General? Well, what are they waiting for? I mean, why have they kept it a secret from us, the members of his household?"

"I cannot . . . Well, actually it hasn't been finally decided. . . . You must know that they are waiting for word from Russia; and then, too, the General has to attend to his business . . ."

"Ah, I see, you mean the old Grandmother?"

Des Grieux looked at me with loathing.

"To be brief," he said, "I am relying fully upon your innate delicacy, tact, and intelligence. . . . I am sure you'll abstain for the sake of the family who have treated you like one of themselves and who all have liked and respected you . . ."

"But how can you say such things, since I've been dismissed! Now you claim that they just pretended to do so; but I suppose you will agree that if I said to you that I certainly had no wish at all to pull your ears, but, just for appearances' sake, would you please allow me to pull them—well, wouldn't you agree that it amounts to the same thing?"

"Well, since it seems to be quite useless to ask you for a favor," he said sternly and offensively, "you may rest assured that appropriate measures will be taken. There are authorities here, and you'll be deported from the principality this very day. *Que diable! Un blanc-bec comme vous* has the pretension to challenge a man of the Baron's importance to a duel! Do you really imagine they'll allow you to go on with this? And take my word for it—no one is afraid of you around here! If I came to talk to you, I did so rather on my own initiative, because the General was worried. And how can you really expect the Baron to do anything else but have you kicked out by his butler?"

"Why, did you think I was going there myself?" I replied with the utmost calm. "Oh no, Monsieur des Grieux, everything will be done in much better form than you imagine. You see, I am going to see Mr. Astley now, to ask him to act as my representative. He is fond of me and I am sure he won't refuse me the favor. He will go to the Baron's, and the Baron will receive him. Now, while I am only a humble tutor, an apparently defenseless subordinate, everyone here knows that Mr. Astley is the nephew of a real lord—Lord Peabroke, who also happens to be here now. Believe me, the Baron will be very polite to Mr. Astley and will receive him. And if, by chance, he doesn't wish to receive him, Mr. Astley will consider it a personal insult—you know how stubborn the English are —and he will send one of his friends to the Baron; he has many worthwhile friends. Now, you understand perhaps that things won't turn out quite the way you were expecting."

The Frenchman was obviously getting cold feet. It all sounded quite plausible, and it may have looked to him at that point as if I really had the means of causing trouble.

"But please, please," he said now in a pleading tone, "don't do that! It looks as if you enjoy trouble, and I'm beginning to think that what you are after is not really an apology, but that you wish simply to stir up a scandal. I told you that it may all be very funny and witty—which is possibly what you want. But to come to the point," he concluded as I stood up and took my hat, ready to leave, "I've come here to give you a message from a certain person—here, read it, for I was asked to wait for an answer."

The following was written in Paulina's hand:

I am under the impression that you intend to go on with this affair. You are angry and so continue to behave like a schoolboy. But there are certain things involved here that one day I may explain to you. And now, please stop it and keep quiet. What nonsense it all is! I need you, and you yourself have promised to obey me. Remember Schlangenberg. I beg, or if I must, order you to obey.

Yours,
P.

P.S. If you are angry with me for what happened yesterday, forgive me.

The room spun before my eyes as I read those lines. My lips turned white and I began to tremble. The damned Frenchman was looking at me with assumed discretion, even pretending to turn his eyes away so as not to see my embarrassment. I would have preferred him to laugh at me openly.

"All right," I replied, "tell Mademoiselle, she needn't

worry. Still," I added sharply, "I'd like to know why it took you so long to give me her note? Instead of talking all sorts of nonsense, it seems to me you should have given it to me right away . . . since that was what she sent you for."

"Oh, I wanted . . . It is all so strange that you must forgive my natural anxiety. I would like to find out from you personally, and as soon as possible, what your intentions are. Actually, I have no idea what is in that note and didn't suppose there was anything particularly urgent about it."

"I understand. You were told to give it to me only if all else failed, and to keep it if you managed to convince me by other means. Isn't that the truth? I want a straight answer, Monsieur des Grieux!"

"*Peut-être,*" he said, looking strangely composed now, and giving me a peculiar glance.

I took my hat, nodded to him, and left. I thought I detected a sarcastic smile on his lips. Well, how could he feel differently?

"You'll pay for that yet, you lousy Frenchie. We'll see which of us has the last laugh," I muttered, rushing downstairs. I was still in a daze, as if I'd received a blow on the head. Outside, though, the fresh air cooled me off a bit.

Then, a couple of minutes later, as soon as I was able to think straight, two things stood out clearly in my mind: one, that all this fuss had arisen from a few threats made by an irresponsible young fellow like me; and two, that this Frenchman must have some sort of influence over Paulina. He says one word and she does exactly what he wants—writes that note and even *begs* me. True, their relations had always been a mystery to me, ever since I first joined the General's family; still, in the past few days I had noticed in her a definite scorn and even revulsion for him, while he plainly avoided looking at her, to a point where his behavior verged on outright rudeness. I'd noticed that. And besides, Paulina herself had

spoken of her disgust. Some important admissions had already escaped her . . . hence, he simply has her under his
control, he holds her shackled in some sort of chains. . . .

VIII

On the promenade, as they refer here to the path under
the chestnut trees, I came across my Englishman.

"Oh, I say," he began when he caught sight of me,
"when you came to see me, I had gone to see you. Have
you already parted from the General?"

"Tell me, first, where did you hear all that?" I asked
in surprise. "Is it known all over the place, then?"

"Oh no, not all over the place. It's not that important.
No one is talking about it."

"So how did you find out?"

"I heard it by chance. And you, where are you going
from here? I like you, and that's why I wanted to see
you."

"You're a fine man, Mr. Astley," I said, still wondering
how he could have found out, "and since I haven't yet
had my coffee and I don't suppose you've had yours, let's
go to the café in the Casino and sit down there and have
a smoke; then I'll tell you everything from the beginning,
and you'll tell me what you know, too."

The café was only about a hundred yards away. They
brought us coffee and I lit a cigarette. Mr. Astley did not
light one, but stared at me and prepared himself to listen.

"I am not going anywhere. I am staying right here," I
began.

While I was on my way to Mr. Astley's, I had had no
intention whatever of telling him anything about my love
for Paulina. In all those days, I had hardly even mentioned her to him. Besides, he was a very shy man. I had
noticed from the beginning how impressed he was by

Paulina, but he never mentioned her name. Strangely, though, no sooner had he installed himself and fixed his heavy, leaden stare on my face, than I suddenly felt, I don't know why, like telling him about my love for her, with all the details and nuances. I went on talking for a full half-hour, and I immensely enjoyed talking about it for the first time ever. And when I noticed that, at the most intimate passages, he looked a bit embarrassed, I deliberately spiced up my narrative. I regret only one thing —I may have said things about the Frenchman I really shouldn't have said. . . .

Mr. Astley listened, sitting in front of me, silent and motionless, and staring straight into my eyes. But when I mentioned the Frenchman, he suddenly interrupted me to ask quite sternly whether I was sure I had the right to bring in "an extraneous circumstance." Mr. Astley always had a strange way of formulating his questions.

"You have a point there," I said. "I may not have the right."

"And you cannot say anything specific about the Marquis and Miss Paulina, aside from your assumptions, can you?"

Once more I was taken aback at such a categorical question coming from such a shy person as Mr. Astley.

"No, nothing specific," I said, "nothing at all."

"If that's so, you have acted improperly, not only in mentioning it to me, but even in assuming such things in your thoughts."

"All right, all right, I admit I was wrong, but that's not what matters most now."

And I went on to tell him about everything that had happened the day before: Paulina's whim, my adventure with the Baron, my dismissal, the General's peculiar fear; and then about Des Grieux's visit to me that morning, in full detail. And, finally, I showed him Paulina's note.

"Well, what do you make of it?" I asked him. "I wanted to see you precisely to know what you thought of it. As for me, I think I'd like to kill that Frenchie and, indeed, I may very well do so."

"I too," Mr. Astley said. "But as to Miss Paulina . . .

well, you know, one may be forced to have contact with people who are most repulsive to one. There may be a connection between them which is unknown to you, and which depends on extraneous circumstances. I think you can set your mind at rest, at least to some extent. Her whim yesterday was, of course, rather strange—not because, wishing to get rid of you, she put you in danger of the Baron's walking stick (and I don't understand why he didn't use it, since he had it handy), but because such a whim is quite unsuitable . . . quite improper, for such a nice young lady. Of course, she couldn't possibly imagine that you would carry out her malicious request to the letter. . . ."

"You know what?" I exclaimed suddenly, looking very closely at Mr. Astley. "I have the impression that you must have heard about all this before! And I know who told you—it was Paulina herself!"

He looked at me in surprise.

"Your eyes are sparkling and I see suspicion in them," he said, recapturing his usual calm; "but you have no right whatever to show it. I, at least, don't acknowledge that right, and I refuse to answer your question."

"All right, all right, you don't have to," I shouted, strangely agitated, and unable to understand how the idea had come into my head. Anyway, when, where, and under what circumstances could Mr. Astley possibly have become Paulina's confidant? But then, I had somewhat lost touch with him, and as to Paulina, she had always been a mystery to me, so that now, when I let myself go and told Mr. Astley all about my love, it suddenly struck me, as I was speaking, that I couldn't say anything precise and specific about my relations with her. Actually our relations were rather fantastic, strange, unreal, unsubstantial, and unlike anything else.

"Well, I admit I am quite confused and cannot think straight now," I said, feeling out of breath. "But I know you are a good man, and what I want from you is not your advice but simply your opinion." I paused for a moment and then went on: "Why do you think the General

73

got so scared? Why did they make all that fuss about a stupid childish prank? Indeed, they blew it up so large that Des Grieux himself found it incumbent upon him to take a hand in it (and he only interferes on the most important occasions), and to come to see me—something, isn't it? He even begged and beseeched me—he, Des Grieux, beseeched me! And please note, he came to see me before nine in the morning and he already had Paulina's note with him. The question is: when was that note written? Perhaps she was waked up for the purpose. Besides, that leads me to the conclusion that Paulina is his slave—she even begs me to forgive her—and, finally, why should *she* worry about it all—I mean, she personally? Why does she take such an interest in this stupid story? Why did they get so frightened of the Baron? And who cares whether the General does or does not marry that Blanche de Cominges? They claim they have to behave with *special* discretion because of that; but isn't it getting too *special* for words, don't you think? I can see by your eyes that you know much more than I do about it all."

Mr. Astley smiled faintly and shook his head.

"Well, I must say, it does look as if I know quite a bit more than you about that too," he said. "The whole thing concerns only Mademoiselle de Cominges, and that is the absolute truth."

"Well, what about Blanche de Cominges?" I asked quickly, feeling suddenly hopeful that he would reveal something about Paulina.

"I have the impression that Mademoiselle Blanche is at present especially interested in avoiding meeting the Baron and Baroness and especially in not being involved in any unpleasantness, or even worse, a scandal with them."

"Go on, go on!"

"Two seasons ago, Mademoiselle Blanche was also in Roulettenburg, and I happened to be here too. At that time, she didn't call herself Mademoiselle de Cominges, and her mother, Madame la veuve Cominges, didn't exist. At least, there was never any mention of her. Des Grieux wasn't around either. I am convinced that they are not only unrelated, but that they haven't known each other for long. And I am certain that he has also only quite recently become a marquis. I have good reason for thinking that. We can even take it for granted that he hasn't been called Des Grieux for very long. I know someone here who knew him under another name."

"But he does have very solid connections, doesn't he?"

"Oh, that's quite possible. Even Mademoiselle Blanche may be well connected. Nevertheless, two years ago, on the request of the Baroness, Mademoiselle Blanche was asked by the local police to leave town, and she left."

"But what had she done?"

"She appeared here first with an Italian, some prince bearing the historic name of Barberini, or something like that. The man was covered with rings and diamonds that weren't even false. They drove out in a splendid carriage. Mademoiselle Blanche played *trente et quarante,* successfully at first, but then her luck ran out—I remember that. I am thinking of one particular evening when she lost a considerable sum. But the worst of it all was that, *un beau matin,* her prince vanished without a trace, and with him went the horses, the carriage, and everything. There was a huge bill left at the hotel. Mademoiselle Zelma—for from Princess Barberini, she had suddenly turned into Mademoiselle Zelma—was in despair. She wailed and screamed so that the whole hotel could hear her, and in her rage she tore her dress. Well, a Polish count (for all traveling Poles are counts) who was staying in the hotel, was greatly impressed by Mademoiselle Zelma, tearing her dress and scratching her face like a she-cat with her beautiful polished nails. They had a little talk and, by lunchtime, she was consoled. In the evening they showed up, arm-in-arm, at the Casino. She was laughing loudly, as usual, and displaying even more freedom of manner than before. She suddenly became one of those gambling ladies who, as they approach the table, think nothing of giving a vigorous shove to a player in order to obtain a spot near the croupier. That is considered very chic among those ladies. I am sure you must have noticed them, haven't you?"

"Yes, yes, of course."

"Well, you couldn't really help noticing them. To the great annoyance of the decent public, that species of woman is nowhere near to becoming extinct here, that is, the kind who can change thousand-franc notes at the roulette table every day. But as soon as they stop changing big notes, they are requested to leave.

"Well, although Mademoiselle Zelma kept changing thousand-franc notes, her playing became less and less successful. Mind you, those ladies are very often successful gamblers, for they have extraordinary control over themselves. But, actually, that's the end of my story. One day, the Count disappeared, just as the Prince had done before. Mademoiselle Zelma appeared in the Casino by herself that evening; this time no one gave her his arm. In two days she lost everything she had. Having played and lost her last louis d'or, she looked around and saw Baron Wurmerhelm near her. He was examining her very attentively and with great indignation. But she missed the indignant part of it and with her famous smile asked him to put ten louis d'or on the red for her. Because of that, following a complaint from the Baroness, she was requested that evening not to appear in the Casino any more. Now, in case you are wondering how I know all these minute and unseemly details, let me explain that I got them from a relative of mine who drove Mademoiselle Zelma from Roulettenburg to Spa that evening.

"Now you'll probably understand why Mademoiselle Blanche wants to marry the General—she'd like not to receive requests to leave, such as she received from the police two years ago. She doesn't gamble any more now, for she has capital and, according to various signs, she lends money to gamblers for interest. That is much more profitable. As a matter of fact, I suspect the poor General owes her quite a bit of money too. Maybe Des Grieux also owes her, although it is quite possible that he is her associate.

So you can understand yourself that, at least until the wedding, she would like very much to avoid attracting the attention of the Baron and Baroness. It amounts to this—in her situation, a public scandal is very much to her disadvantage. And so, as long as you were connected with the General's household, your involvement was bound to attract attention to her, inasmuch as she is to be seen in public every day, arm-in-arm with the General or with Miss Paulina. Now, I suppose you understand?"

"No, I do not!" I shouted at the top of my voice, banging the table with my fist so violently that a frightened waiter came rushing over to us.

"Tell me, Mr. Astley," I said, still in a fit of rage, "since you already knew all these things and therefore were fully aware of what sort of a person that Blanche de Cominges is, why didn't you at least warn me or, better still, the General himself and, above all, Paulina, who shows herself in the Casino and other public places arm-in-arm with that woman?"

"There was no point in my warning you, since you couldn't do a thing about it," Mr. Astley said phlegmatically; "and anyway, what was there to warn you about? Perhaps the General knows much more about Mademoiselle Blanche than I do, but even so, that would hardly stop him from appearing in public places with her, or even allowing Miss Paulina to do so. I saw Mademoiselle Blanche on a magnificent horse yesterday, riding in the company of Des Grieux and that little Russian Prince, with the General following them on a roan horse. In the morning he had been complaining that his legs ached, but he sat his horse well. And it suddenly occurred to me that he was a completely lost man. But, of course, none of this is my business, and it is only recently that I have come to know Miss Paulina. And anyway," Mr. Astley said, seeming to be suddenly afraid he had said too much, "I have already told you that I cannot recognize your right to ask certain questions, although I am very fond of you. . . ."

"That's enough," I said, standing up; "now it is obvious to me that Paulina, too, knows everything about Mademoiselle Blanche, but that she cannot give up her Frenchman, and so allows herself to be seen in town in that woman's company. Believe me, no other consideration would have made her walk arm-in-arm with Mademoiselle Blanche and beseech me in that note to leave the Baron in peace. Yes, I am sure Des Grieux has some power over her and that she has no choice but to submit. But then, it was she who set me on the Baron in the first place. . . . Oh hell, I can't make any sense out of it, after all."

"You are forgetting two things: one, that this Blanche de Cominges is the General's fiancée; and two, that the General has, besides his stepdaughter Miss Paulina, a small boy and a girl, his own children, who have been completely neglected by that crazy man and whom, I believe, he has completely ruined."

"Yes, yes, that's quite true! Leaving would amount to deserting the children; remaining here makes it possible to defend their interests and perhaps even to save at least a few crumbs from the estate. Yes, yes, all that is very true. But still . . . Ah, now I understand why it is they are all taking so much interest in the Grandmother just now!"

"Interest in whom?" Mr. Astley asked.

"In that old witch in Moscow. They are expecting a telegram announcing her death, but she keeps refusing to die."

"Yes, of course, all their interest is centered on her. It's all about her will: if it is found that she has left a substantial fortune, the General will marry, Miss Paulina's hands will be untied, and Des Grieux . . ."

"And what about Des Grieux?"

"He will be paid. That's all he's waiting for."

"That's all? You don't think he's waiting for something else?"

"I don't know anything more about it," Mr. Astley said doggedly.

"But I do, I do know!" I cried furiously. "He too is waiting for the inheritance, for Paulina will then get a dowry and, once she has the money, she will throw herself on his neck. All women are like that! Even the proudest of them are likely to turn into vulgar slaves! All Paulina is capable of is passionate love; outside of that—nothing! That's what I think of her! Just look at her when she is alone and thinks she is unobserved—there is something doomed, predestined, and damned about her. She is made for suffering all the horrors of life, for experiencing all the passions . . . she . . . But who is that calling me? Who is that shouting? I heard a Russian voice call 'Alexei, Alexei!' A woman calling me . . . Can you hear?"

At that moment we were approaching my hotel. We had left the café and had been walking for quite a while without really noticing.

"I heard a woman's voice shouting, but I can't make it out; yes, it sounds like Russian. Wait, now I see where it's coming from," Mr. Astley said, pointing to the entrance of the hotel. "It's that woman shouting—see, the one sitting in that big wheel chair, who is now being carried through the door by the servants. They are carrying her luggage in behind her. That means a train has just come in."

"But why was she calling me? Listen, she's shouting again . . . Look, she's waving to us."

"Yes, I see her waving," Mr. Astley said.

"Alexei! Can't you hear me, Alexei! Ah, good Lord, what a stupid fellow!" I heard the frantic shouts coming from the hotel lobby.

We ran all the way to the entrance door. I went in, and my hands fell to my sides in amazement, while my feet felt as if they were rooted in the ground.

IX

Reclining in the wheel chair in which she had been carried in by footmen, surrounded by chambermaids, waiters, and all sorts of flunkeys, and the hotel manager himself, who had come to greet this honored guest who had arrived with so much fanfare, with her own retinue and an impressive array of suitcases and trunks, the Grandmother was lording it over the main lobby of the hotel.

Yes, it was the Grandmother in person, the dreaded, wealthy, seventy-five-year-old Antonida Vasilievna Tarasevich, a big landowner, a Moscow lady, the "Grandma" about whom so many telegrams had been sent and received, the dying-but-not-yet-dead old woman who had now descended on us like a bolt out of the blue. Although she was deprived of the use of her legs and was transported in her wheel chair, as she had been for the past five years, she was her old self—alert, aggressive, self-satisfied, straight-backed, shouting at everyone in a loud and imperious voice, abusing those who displeased her—in short, exactly the same as when I had had the honor of seeing her on two occasions since I had become a tutor in the General's family.

I stood in front of her, completely nonplused. Her lynx's eye had recognized me from a hundred yards away, while she was being carried through the hotel door, and she had started calling out my name, for she always remembered people's names.

And to think they had believed she would be dead and buried by now and they would be dividing up her estate! Well, it seemed much more likely that it would be she who'd bury the lot of us. But what would happen to the others? What would the General do? The old lady would turn the whole place upside down now, I thought.

"Well, why are you staring at me like that, young fellow?" she shouted at me. "Don't you have any manners? You could at least say you're pleased to see me. What is it? Have you become too proud, or what? Perhaps you don't recognize me? Look at him, Potapych," she said, turning to her majordomo, a small gray old man with a pink bald spot, "he doesn't recognize me! You'd think they'd buried me for good! The way they sent cable after cable asking is she dead or isn't she! Ah, I know all about it. And, as you can see for yourself, I'm still alive and kicking."

"Please, ma'am, why should I wish you ill?" I replied in a cheerful tone, having recovered from my surprise. "It's true, though, that this is quite a surprise for me. . . . Well, how could I help being surprised? It's so unexpected . . ."

"But why should you be surprised, my lad? I just took the train and came. It is quite comfortable in the train, doesn't shake you too much. . . . And you, where have you come from now—have you been out for a walk, or what?"

"Yes, I went to the Casino for a bit."

"It's nice here," the Grandmother said. "It's warm, and the trees are beautiful. I like that. The General and the rest are in, aren't they?"

"They must be in at this hour."

"So they have fixed hours here too, and keep up all that fuss! Trying to keep up appearances, eh? I understand they keep a carriage and play the part of *les seigneurs russes!* They lost all they had, and off they went abroad! Is Paulina here too?"

"Yes, Paulina's here too."

"And that little Frenchie too, I suppose? Well, I'll see them all soon enough for myself. So go ahead, Alexei, lead me straight to the General. But tell me, do you like it here?"

"So-so, ma'am."

"Now you, Potapych, tell that stupid hotel manager to get me a decent suite. And not too high up. Have the things carried up there right away. But I don't need all these people to carry me! What a lot of flunkeys! Tell them to keep away. Who is this fellow with you?" she asked, turning to me again.

"This is Mr. Astley."

"And who is Mr. Astley?"

"A visitor here, a good friend of mine. He also knows the General."

"He must be English, judging by the way he's staring at me without opening his mouth. But I like the English, after all. All right then, carry me upstairs—straight to the General's suite. Well, where is it?"

They lifted the old lady and I preceded her up the broad staircase. It was a very impressive cortege indeed, and everyone who happened to be there stopped and stared, open-mouthed. Our hotel was considered the best, the most expensive, and the most aristocratic in the resort. One was almost always sure to come across fine ladies and important-looking Englishmen in the lobby and in the corridors. Many people inquired about the old lady from the manager, who was very much impressed himself. He, of course, told the curious that the important foreign visitor was *une russe, une comtesse, une grande dame,* and that she was to occupy the suite that had been vacated last week by *la grande-duchesse de N.* For the most part this impression was due to the Grandmother's imperious and imposing bearing, as she was carried in her wheel chair. When she saw a new face, she appraised it with curiosity, loudly questioning me. The Grandmother was a big woman, and although she never left her wheel chair it was easy to guess that she was very tall. Her back was as straight as a board, and she held her big gray head high. Her features were large and marked, and there was something aggressive and challenging in her gaze. It was obvious that both her expression and her gestures were completely unaffected. Despite her seventy-five years, her face did not look old, and even her teeth were still very good. She wore a black silk dress and a white bonnet.

"I find her fascinating," Mr. Astley whispered in my ear as he walked along beside me.

She knows about the telegrams and about Des Grieux, I thought, but it is unlikely that she would know much about Blanche. And immediately I shared this thought with Mr. Astley.

I must confess that, once I got over my first surprise, I relished the thought of the shock the sight of us would give the General. I was very excited at the idea, and led the procession quite cheerfully.

The General's suite was on the third floor. I hadn't sent anyone to announce us, and didn't even knock at the door

—I just pushed it wide open and the old lady was triumphantly ushered in.

And, as though to order, they were all assembled in the General's study. It was about midday, and I believe they were planning to go on an excursion out of town, some on horseback, some in carriages. Some acquaintances had been invited to go along. Besides the General, Paulina, and the children with their nurse, there were present in the study Des Grieux, Mademoiselle Blanche in her riding habit, her mother, Madame Veuve de Cominges, the little Prince, and some learned German traveler whom I saw with them for the first time.

The Grandmother's wheel chair was set down in the middle of the room, three steps from the General. Ah, I'll never forget the sight! Just as we came in, the General had been saying something, while Des Grieux kept correcting him. It must be said that for the last three days both Des Grieux and Blanche had been making a great fuss over the little Prince, *à la barbe du pauvre général*. The prevailing atmosphere in the room, although it may have been forced, was cheerful and intimate.

When he saw the old lady, the General fell silent in the middle of a word and stood there petrified, with his mouth wide open. He stared at her with bulging eyes, as if spellbound by a serpent. And she too remained immobile, staring back at him, and what a triumphant and sarcastic look it was!

And so they remained, their eyes fixed on each other in dead silence for perhaps ten seconds. Des Grieux, who had been paralyzed at first, soon snapped out of it, and a very worried expression appeared on his face. Mademoiselle Blanche examined the old lady with raised eyebrows. The little Prince and the learned German looked around, completely bewildered. Anger and surprise showed in Paulina's eyes; she suddenly went deadly pale, but a moment later the blood returned to her face and her cheeks flushed. Yes, it was a catastrophe for all of them! And so I kept shifting my eyes from the Grandmother to everyone else in the room, and back again. Mr. Astley, in keeping with his usual good manners, stood discreetly and inconspicuously in a corner.

"Well, here I am. I've come in person, instead of a telegram!" the old lady roared, at last breaking the silence. "You didn't expect me, did you?"

"Auntie Antonida, dear . . . How . . . how did you . . ." the poor General mumbled helplessly, and I believed if she had waited any longer before saying something, he'd have suffered a stroke.

"What do you mean, how? What do you think the railroads are for? I just got into the train and came. And you were all imagining I'd died and left you all my possessions? Why, I know all about the telegrams you kept sending. I can imagine what a lot of money you spent on them, for it can't be too cheap to send a telegram from here, is it? And anyway, they must have overcharged you. And so I just decided to come, and here I am! And is this that Frenchman—Des Grieux, I believe?"

"*Oui, madame,*" Des Grieux said, "*et croyez, je suis si enchanté . . . votre sante . . . c'est un miracle . . . vous voir ici . . . une surprise charmante . . .*"

"I can believe it's *une surprise charmante.* I know you, you fake, and I wouldn't trust you with that, even." She marked off a tiny bit on her little finger. "And who is she?" the old lady said, pointing to Blanche, for the handsome Frenchwoman in riding habit and with a whip in her hand had obviously rather impressed her. "Does she come from around here?"

"This is Mademoiselle Blanche de Cominges, and this is her mother, Madame de Cominges. They are staying at this hotel," I informed her.

"Is the daughter married?" the old lady asked unabashedly.

"No, she is single," I answered most discreetly, in a very hushed tone.

"Is she fun?" And as I hadn't understood her question, she elaborated: "I mean, it must be possible to have a good time with her. Does she understand Russian? Des Grieux, for instance, managed to pick up some Russian while he was in Moscow."

I told her that Mademoiselle de Cominges had never been to Russia.

"*Bonjour!*" the Grandmother said then, abruptly turning toward Blanche.

"*Bonjour, madame,*" Blanche responded with a graceful curtsy, trying under cover of great discretion and politeness to express with her face and body her extreme surprise at such a strange address.

"Look at that—she's lowered her eyes and is making faces and putting on delicate airs! I know that sort so well—she must be an actress or something. . . . I've got myself a suite downstairs in this hotel," she said, turning abruptly toward the General. "So we'll be neighbors now, whether you like it or not."

"Oh, Auntie, I wish you would believe how sincerely I feel . . . how delighted I am," the General said hurriedly. He had recovered by now, and since he felt that on occasion he could express himself effectively, eloquently, and with considerable dignity, he was trying to make use of his gifts right now. "We were all of us shocked and alarmed by the news of your illness. . . . We received such hopeless telegrams . . . and now, suddenly—"

"Come, come, stop lying!" the Grandmother interrupted.

"But how is it," the General interrupted her in his turn, trying to ignore what she had said, "how is it, Auntie, that you decided to come on such a trip? You must agree that, at your age, and in your state of health . . . Well, at least your coming is so unexpected that our surprise is quite understandable. But I am awfully pleased you've come, and we will all," he said, with an ecstatic and tender smile, "do our best to make your stay here as pleasant as possible."

"All right, enough of this empty talk. You're still as full of wind as ever, I see; but, don't worry, I'm quite sure I'll be able to take care of myself here. And don't go imagining I'm angry with you now—I don't hold grudges. You were asking, how is it I could come? Well, the answer is: It was very simple. And why should you all be so surprised? Hello, Paulina! How are you getting along here?"

"Hello, Grandmother," Paulina said, going over to her. "Have you been on the way long?"

"Well, you at least sound more intelligent than the others—you have the sense to inquire, while they just let out their 'ahs!' and 'ohs!' You see, I was lying in bed, being treated by the doctors, and then I got fed up, kicked the doctors out, and called the sacristan of Saint Nicholas' church. He had cured a peasant woman of a similar illness with herbs. Well, he helped me too, for after two days of his treament I began to sweat, and then felt better and got up. Then my German doctors gathered around again, put on their glasses, and started buzzing away. 'What about going abroad to a spa now,' they said, 'and taking a cure? That would take care of all your pains.' And why not, I said to myself. Then some stupid people started exclaiming: 'You'd never get there in your state!' 'Is that so?' I said. Well, I got ready in one day, took along my maid and Potapych and Fyodor the footman, but I sent Fyodor back from Berlin, because I really didn't have any need for him. In fact, I could have come here all by myself. I had a compartment reserved for me and there are porters at every station—they'd have carried me anywhere for a few kopeks. Ah, you've certainly got yourself a nice place to live here!" she remarked unexpectedly, looking around. "Where did you get the money to pay for all this, my boy? And I thought everything you had was mortgaged! I understand you owe plenty to that Frenchie alone. I know everything, remember, everything!"

"You see, Auntie . . ." the General muttered, greatly embarrassed. "I am surprised at you . . . I thought I could look after my affairs without being controlled. . . . Anyway, my expenses don't exceed my income, and here . . ."

"They don't exceed it? What are you trying to tell me? I'm sure you've quite ruined your children—you, their guardian!"

"If you say things like that . . . I really don't know what . . ." The General mumbled indignantly.

"So you don't know, don't you? Well, I, for my part, would guess that you never leave the roulette table here for very long. Tell me, have you lost everything by now?"

The General was so shocked that he almost choked in an overflow of varied emotions.

"Play roulette? Me? In my position? Come to your senses, dear Aunt, you can't be feeling well."

"I know very well that you're lying, and that they can't drag you away from the roulette table. Tonight I'll have a look and see for myself what that roulette is like. You, Paulina, come and tell me what there is to see here in this town. . . . Yes, and you, Alexei, will accompany me. Here, Potapych, I want you to write down the names of the spots we must see. Well, what is there of interest?" she asked, turning back to Paulina.

"There are the ruins of a castle not far from here. . . . And then, there is, of course, the Schlangenberg. . . ."

"What's the Schlangenberg? A forest or something?"

"No, it's a mountain, and it has a *pointe* . . ."

"What do you mean by a *pointe?*"

"The highest spot of the mountain. It has a railing around it, and the view from it is really wonderful."

"Carry me up to the top of the mountain in my wheel chair? Do you think they'd manage to get me up there?"

"Oh, I'm sure enough porters could be found," I said.

At that moment Fedosia, the nurse, brought the General's children to greet the old lady.

"No, no! No kissing, please! I hate kissing children— their noses are always wet and runny. Well, how do you like it here, Fedosia?"

"It's very, very nice here, ma'am," the nurse said. "But you, ma'am, how is your health? We were really worried about you here."

"I know, I know, and you, at least, you're a simple soul," the old lady said. And then, turning to Paulina again, she asked: "And who are these people? Guests? Who's that little shrimp with the glasses?"

"That's Prince Nilsky, Granny," Paulina whispered.

"Oh, he's Russian . . . I thought he wouldn't understand. Well, perhaps he didn't hear. Where is Mr. Astley? I've seen him already. . . . Ah, there he is! How do you do!" she suddenly shouted to him.

Mr. Astley bowed to her without speaking.

"Well, don't you have anything nice to say to me? Go on, say something! Translate that to him, Paulina."

Paulina did so, and Mr. Astley willingly obliged.

"I am delighted to meet you, and am very happy to see you are in good health," he said, sounding very sincere.

"The English always have the proper answer for everything!" the old lady commented. "I don't know why, but I have always liked the English—they're so incomparably better than those Frenchies! Please come and see me some time," she said, looking at Mr. Astley, "and I'll do my best not to bore you too much. Translate that to him, Paulina, and tell him I am in a first-floor suite here—do you understand? Downstairs—downstairs," she repeated, pointing her finger at the floor and trying to communicate directly with Mr. Astley.

Mr. Astley declared that he would be delighted to come.

Then the old lady took a long, satisfied look at Paulina.

"I could have liked you a lot, Paulina," she declared unexpectedly. "You're a good lass, much better than the rest of them—but what a nasty disposition! But then, I have a nasty disposition myself. . . . Well, turn round a bit. What's that on your head? A false chignon?"

"No, Granny, it's my own hair."

"I'm glad to hear it. I hate today's stupid fashion. I must say, you're very pretty. In fact, if I were a young man I'm sure I'd have fallen head over heels in love with you. Why don't you get married? . . . But I suppose I'd better get out of here now—I need some fresh air, for I've been locked up long enough in that railway carriage. . . . And you," she said, turning to the General, "still furious with me?"

"Oh no, Auntie, why should I be?" the General exclaimed with relief. "I appreciate very well that, at your age . . ."

"*Cette vieille est tombée en enfance,*" Des Grieux whispered in my ear.

"I want to see everything there is to see here," the old lady informed the General, "and I'd like Alexei to accompany me, if you'll let me have him."

"Oh, certainly, of course. . . . But I'd like myself . . . and Paulina . . . and Monsieur des Grieux . . . we'd be very happy, all of us, to accompany you. . . ."

"*Mais, madame, cela sera un plaisir,*" Des Grieux lisped, with a disarming smile.

"Oh, I know—it'd be a *plaisir*. . . . You make me laugh, my dear man. Still, I won't give you any money, you know," she said unexpectedly to the General. "Well, I want to be carried to my suite now. I must have a look at it, then we'll make the round of the place. All right, then, let's get started. Lift me!"

They lifted the old lady in her wheel chair again and everyone followed her downstairs. The General looked stunned as he walked down. Des Grieux was deep in some calculations. Blanche, who at first had decided to stay upstairs, changed her mind at the last moment and joined the others. Prince Nilsky followed her and, seconds later, there was only Madame Veuve de Cominges left in the General's suite.

X

In resorts, and all over Europe generally, hotel managers are less guided by the wishes and requirements of their clients in assigning them suites, than by their own intuition; and it must be said they seldom go wrong. In the old lady's case, however, the manager had perhaps slightly overestimated her position in alloting such a palatial suite to her. It consisted of four magnificently furnished rooms, a bathroom, a pantry, a separate room for her maid, and so on. Actually, a week earlier some grand duchess had stayed in it, a fact that was, of course, immediately told to the new occupants, in order to raise the price even higher. They wheeled the Grandmother around to show her the suite, and she scrutinized everything with an alert and critical eye. The manager, an elderly, balding man, walked respectfully at her side on this first inspection tour.

I don't know who they thought the Grandmother was, but they certainly must have taken her for a very important and, above all, a very wealthy person. They had registered her as *Madame la générale princesse de Tarasevich*, though the Grandmother had never been a princess. It must have been the fact that she was traveling with her own servants and that she had come with an incredible array of useless luggage, including several trunks, that first gave the old lady her prestige. And then, her wheel chair, her imperious voice, her eccentric questions, asked quite unabashedly, her tone that there was no gainsaying, indeed her whole personality—straightforward, impatient, and domineering—put the finishing touches to the feeling of awe she spread around her. During her inspection tour she would suddenly order those wheeling her to halt and, pointing at some piece of furniture, would ask quite unexpected questions of the sheepishly smiling hotel manager, who gradually grew more and more ill at ease. The Grandmother asked her questions in French, which, by the way, she spoke rather poorly, so that I had mostly to repeat them. And then, she disliked most of the man's answers, finding them unsatisfactory. She made it rather difficult for him, since her questions didn't seem to have anything to do with the matter at hand, but were prompted by God knows what. At one point, for instance, she had them stop her chair in front of a painting—a rather mediocre copy of some famous original with a mythological setting.

"Who is the woman in that picture?"

The manager said he thought it was the portrait of some countess.

"How is it you don't know? You live here, and aren't sure what it is? Why is the thing here? Why is she squint-eyed?"

The manager, quite unable to answer these questions, looked at a loss.

"What a fathead!" the Grandmother commented in Russian, and the procession went on.

A similar scene was repeated by a Dresden statuette that the Grandmother examined for a long time and then, for some unspecified reason, ordered to be removed. Then she insisted that the manager tell her how much the carpets in the bedroom were worth and where they had been made. He promised to get her the information.

"What idiots," the old lady said, and started inspecting her bed.

"What a sumptuous bedspread! Open it up." They did so. "Go on, open it up more than that. Take the pillows off. Remove the pillowcases. Lift the comforter."

They turned everything inside out. Grandma watched very attentively.

"A good thing they have no bedbugs. Still, I want them to remove all the bedclothes and replace them with my own. I want my own pillows too. Well, it's a bit big for me—what do I need all this for? I'll feel lost here, lonely old woman that I am. I'll get bored. Do you know what, Alexei—you must come and see me very often. Come whenever you're not busy with the children."

"Since yesterday, I haven't been in the General's service," I said. "I am living in this hotel quite independently from him."

"How's that?"

"Recently a very famous German Baron came to stay here with his Baroness. Well, I met them in the park and spoke to them in none too elegant Berlin German."

91

"So?"

"He took it as insolence and complained to the General, who dismissed me yesterday."

"What did you do? Did you call the Baron names? And even supposing you did, I don't see any harm in that."

"Oh no, rather the other way round—it was the Baron who raised his stick to me."

"And you, you wet nose, you allow people to treat your children's tutor like that!" she said, turning abruptly to the General. "And instead of doing something about it, you just discharged the lad! Ah, what wet chickens you are, my friends, real wet hens!"

"Don't worry about me, Auntie," the General replied with a certain haughty familiarity. "I know how to conduct myself. Besides, Alexei didn't give you an accurate account of what really happened."

"And you, you just took it?" she asked me.

"I wanted to challenge the Baron to a duel," I said quietly, trying to sound as modest as possible, "but the General forbade me."

"Why did you forbid him, now?" the Grandmother said, turning to the General again. "And you, fellow," she said, turning quickly to the manager, "no need for you to stand there open-mouthed—go, and I'll have you called if I need you. . . . I can't stand that Nuremberg face of his!"

The manager bowed and left.

"What are you talking about, Auntie?" the General said with a sarcastic smile. "How would a duel be possible?"

"And why shouldn't it be? Men are all like so many roosters, so let them fight. But you, you are wet chickens, and you're no credit at all to your country. Now, come on, lift me up! Potapych, there must always be two porters standing by to take me around. Go and hire some and see to it. No need for more than two at a time—they'll only have to carry me up and downstairs; in the street, they can roll me. Explain that to them and pay them in advance—that will make them more respectful. You, Potapych, I want to have you always by my side. And you, Alexei, I want you to point out that Baron to me when we meet him. I'd like to have a look at that German. And now, where's the roulette?"

I explained to her that the roulette tables were installed in the Casino's special rooms. Then she asked me how many roulette wheels there were, whether many people played, whether the game went on all day long, how roulette was played. I suggested that the best thing would be for her to have a look at the roulette tables for herself, because it was difficult for me to explain it all to her just like that.

"So, they can take me there right away! You lead the way, Alexei!"

"Why, Auntie, aren't you even going to have a little rest after your long journey?" the General asked solicitously.

He seemed rather agitated, and, in fact, they all appeared quite at a loss and kept exchanging inquiring glances. They were obviously rather reluctant to accompany the old lady to the Casino, where she was likely to keep up her eccentric behavior in public and cause them considerable embarrassment. But despite that, they all offered to accompany her.

"Rest? Why should I? I'm not tired—I've sat without budging for several days. And then we must go and find the mineral springs they have here. I must have a look at them. And then, then . . . what did you call that thing, Paulina? Ah, *pointe,* wasn't it?"

"*Pointe,* that's right, Granny."

"All right, so let's see the *pointe.* And what else is there?"

"There are many things here, Granny," Paulina said, trying to think.

"All right, I see you don't know yourself. . . . You, Martha," the old lady said to her maid, "you're coming with me too."

"But why must you drag her along too, Auntie?" the General protested, sounding quite worried. "No, that's forbidden, after all. And I doubt very much that they'll let Potapych into the Casino either."

"Nonsense! The fact that Martha is a servant is no reason for me to abandon her—she's just as much a real human being as anyone else. We've been on the move for days on end and it's only natural if she wants to have a look around too. And with whom, if not with me, can she go out visiting the place? By herself she wouldn't even show her nose in the street."

"But, Auntie!"

"Why, it sounds as if you were ashamed of me? So why don't you just stay home? No one's insisting on your coming. You think you're too high and mighty because you're a general? That doesn't impress me, and you should know better—I was married to a general, after all. Anyway, why are there so many of you trailing behind me like a tail? I'd rather go around with just Alexei."

But Des Grieux insisted that everyone should come along, choosing some of his most amiable phrases about the joy of being with her, and so on. And the whole party set out.

"Elle est tombée en enfance," Des Grieux kept repeating to the General; *"seule, elle fera des bêtises . . ."*

I didn't catch what else he said, but he obviously had some plan of action, and perhaps his hopes had been restored.

It was less than half a mile to the Casino. We had to follow the chestnut-bordered avenue, then pass a public garden before getting to the Casino. The General seemed a little reassured, for although our procession was rather unusual, it was nevertheless quite proper and dignified. Actually, there was nothing so remarkable about it, for why should it be so exceptional for a sick lady who is unable to use her own legs to come to a health resort? But obviously the General was particularly apprehensive of what would happen in the Casino: why should an invalid without use of her legs, and what's more, an old lady, play roulette?

Paulina and Blanche walked on either side of the wheel chair. Blanche was laughing, with an air that was both cheerful and discreet, and tried very amiably to amuse the Grandmother, for which the old lady finally expressed her appreciation. Paulina, on the other hand, was constantly forced to answer questions thrown at her without let-up, such as: "Who was that person we just passed?" "Who is that woman in the carriage?" "How large is this town?" "Is this garden very big?" "What kind of trees are those?" "What's the name of those mountains?" "Are there any eagles around here?" "What is that funny roof over there?"

Mr. Astley, who was walking at my side, whispered to me that he was expecting a lot from the day. Potapych and Martha were walking directly behind the wheel chair —he in frockcoat and white tie topped by an incongruous cloth cap; she, a forty-year-old, red-cheeked spinster already turning gray, in a calico dress, a white bonnet, and creaking shoes. The Grandmother often turned back to speak to them. The General and Des Grieux had fallen a bit behind and were having an apparently heated conversation. Des Grieux, looking quite determined, was probably trying to give courage to the dejected General, and was giving him some advice. But the old lady had already pronounced the fatal words—she wasn't going to give any money to the General. To Des Grieux, that must have seemed too incredible to believe; but not to the General —he knew his aunt well. I also noticed that Des Grieux and Blanche kept exchanging significant looks. As to the Russian Prince and the German traveler, I caught sight of them at the end of the avenue—they fell behind and then disappeared somewhere.

Our arrival at the Casino was a triumph. The doorman and the flunkeys displayed the same respect as the staff of the hotel, although they did look at us with curiosity. To start with, the Grandmother wanted to be wheeled through all the rooms in the Casino—she praised certain things, coldly disapproved of others, asked many questions. When we finally reached the roulette rooms, the lackey who stood before the closed door like a sentry took one look at the old lady and, as though overcome with awe, flung it wide open.

The Grandmother made a sensation when she appeared

in the room. At the roulette tables and at the opposite end of the room, where *trente et quarante* was played, there must have been a good hundred and fifty or even two hundred players, crowded in several rows. Those who had managed to get right up to the tables, held their ground with determination, refusing to budge until they had lost all they had on them, for to stand there as ordinary onlookers was not allowed. And although chairs were placed around the table, very few gamblers sat down when there were many people around, because it was much easier to get close to the table if one was standing up and much easier to place one's stakes from that position. The second and third rows watched and waited, eager to be the first to get there when a spot at the table was vacant. And they were so impatient that, now and then, a hand would shoot out over the shoulders of the human hedge and deposit its ante. Even those in the third row occasionally managed to place stakes in this way, and this caused an "incident" every five or ten minutes, because different people claimed to have placed the same stake. But it must be said that the Casino police were very efficient. The establishment could not, of course, avoid crowding; on the contrary, the more people there were the better they liked it, because that meant bigger profits. But the eight croupiers kept a careful eye on the stakes, paid out the winnings, and if an argument arose, it was they who decided the issue. In extreme cases, however, they called in the police, and within a minute the incident was closed.

The police wear mufti and mingle with the public, so that it is quite impossible to recognize them. They mostly keep their eyes open for small-time thieves and professional crooks, of whom there are a great many around, for they find the gambling rooms the most convenient place for the practice of their trade. Indeed, elsewhere they have to steal from people's pockets or break into locked premises—ventures that, if unsuccessful, land them in a lot of trouble—while here, all they have to do is to walk up to the roulette table, place a small stake, and then quite brazenly and openly pick up someone else's winnings and put them in their pockets. And if an argument starts, the crook can loudly insist that the stake was definitely his. If he does so cleverly enough, the witnesses begin to hesitate, and the thief may manage to hold on to the money, but only, of course, if the disputed sum is not too substantial. If it is very big, the croupiers or some of the others are certain to have noticed it. On the other hand, if the sum is quite insignificant, its rightful owner often does not even wish to get into a public argument about it, and so gives it up. But whenever a thief is caught red-handed, he is always ignominiously ejected.

The Grandmother watched all this from a distance with tremendous curiosity, and was very amused to see the thieves thrown out. She was quite indifferent to *trente et quarante*, but roulette with its little ball spinning round caught her imagination. After a while she expressed a wish to become better acquainted with the game. I don't know exactly how it happened, but the flunkeys and certain servile characters—mostly the nondescript Poles, who, having lost everything, thrust their services upon lucky gamblers and any prosperous-looking foreigner—immediately managed to have a place cleared at the table, near the chief croupier, and wheeled her up to it in her chair. Many people who were not playing, but only watching the game (mostly Englishmen with their families), immediately moved over to the table to get a glimpse of the old lady over the human barrier. Many a lorgnette was directed toward her. The croupier's hopes went up, for such an eccentric gambler seemed to hold promise that there might be big action. It was certainly not a daily occurrence to find a seventy-five-year-old grandmother, confined to a wheel chair, going in for gambling. I pushed my way to the table, too, and stationed myself at the Grandmother's elbow. Potapych and Martha were left behind somewhere in the crowd. The General, Paulina, Des Grieux, and Mademoiselle Blanche stood to one side with the other onlookers.

The old lady began by examining the players around her, asking me terse, direct questions in a half-whisper:

Who's he? Who's she? She took a special fancy to a young man who was playing for very large stakes, and who had already—according to the whispers of the audience—won something in the vicinity of forty thousand francs. The money lay before him in a pile of gold coins and thousand-franc notes. He was very pale, his eyes glistened, his hands trembled. He had stopped counting his stakes, and would just take a handful of money and toss it on the table, and still he kept winning and winning and raking in his gains. Flunkeys kept bustling around him, pushing an armchair under him and clearing space about him to give him more room—all in the hope of a rich man's appreciation, for some gamblers are so happy to win that, when they do, they hand money out by the handful, without counting it. A Pole had already installed himself near the young man and kept whispering something in his ear with an excited but at the same time servile expression on his face; he was probably advising him where to place his stakes and how to play, simply in the hope of getting a hand-out eventually. But the gambler ignored the Pole almost entirely and kept betting haphazardly and raking in his winnings. He had apparently lost his head completely.

The Grandmother watched him for a few minutes. Then she suddenly gave me a big poke and, looking very agitated, said:

"Tell him to stop now. . . . Tell him to take his money and get out of here. He's about to lose everything," she whispered, almost choking with emotion. "Where's Potapych? Send Potapych to him! Well, go on, tell him, tell him!" She kept nudging me. "But where's Potapych, after all? *Sortez, sortez!*" she cried, trying to communicate directly with the young man.

I whispered in her ear that it was strictly forbidden to shout there, and that, as a matter of fact, we weren't even supposed to talk in loud voices, because it made the counting of money difficult; and that if she went on like that, they'd throw us out.

"What a shame! That boy is lost! Well, he's asking for

it! I can't watch it—it upsets me so! What an idiot!" And she tried to look the other way.

On the Grandmother's left, at the other end of the table, there was a young lady sitting next to a dwarf. Who the dwarf was—a relative of hers, or simply someone she brought with her for effect, I cannot say. I had noticed the lady before: she showed up at the roulette table every day at one o'clock and left at two sharp, always playing for exactly one hour. She was already well known there, and as soon as she appeared an armchair was rolled up for her. She took out some gold pieces and a few thousand-franc notes and played calmly, coolly, calculatingly, writing down the winning numbers on a piece of paper and trying to discover the pattern in which the numbers were coming up that day. She played for rather large stakes. In a day, she would win one, two, or three thousand francs, no more, and then she would leave while she was ahead. The Grandmother watched her closely.

"That one—she won't lose! That type never loses. What nationality is she, have you any idea?"

"She must be French," I whispered. "One of that sort, you know."

"I can tell the bird by the way it flies, and I can see that her talons are sharp. Now, explain to me, what does each turn of the wheel mean? What's the right way to play?"

I did my best to explain to her the various possible plays, *rouge et noir, pair et impair, manque et passe,* and, finally, the various nuances in the patterns of numbers. She listened attentively, asked me to repeat, tried to remember it all by heart. There were plenty of opportunities there for me to illustrate every system of placing stakes, and so she learned quickly and effortlessly. She was very pleased with the lesson.

"And what if it's the zero that comes up? That chief croupier, the curly-haired one, shouted *'zéro!'* just now. Why did he take everything there was on the table? And it was a pretty neat pile he raked in, too! How is that?"

"Well, when the zero comes up, everything on the table goes to the bank."

"Is that so! So I can never get a thing when the zero comes up?"

"Well, that's not quite so: if you played the zero yourself, you'd receive thirty-five times the amount you played."

"What! Thirty-five times? But it seems to come up quite often. So why don't these fools play it?"

"Because it's a thirty-six to one chance, ma'am."

"Nonsense, nonsense. . . . Hey, Potapych! But wait, I have some money on me. Here!" She took out a fat purse, extracted a ten-gulden piece from it, and handed it to me. "Here, put it on the zero."

"But, ma'am, the zero has only just come up," I said, "and so it won't come up again for a long time. You'd better wait for a while before playing it."

"Nonsense. Put it on the zero right away."

"Just as you please, but it may not come up at all until evening. You may play it a thousand times without its coming up."

"Nonsense! Sheer nonsense! If you're afraid of wolves, you'll never go into the forest. What? We've lost it? Put another one on it!"

We lost the second ten-gulden piece too, and played a third. The old lady could hardly keep her place as she gazed intently at the little ball bouncing in the notches of the revolving wheel. And the third coin went the way of the first two. She became furious, twisted in her chair, and even banged her fist on the table when the croupier announced *"trente-six"* instead of the *"zéro"* she was waiting for.

"Oh!" she fumed. "What is it waiting for, that miserable little zero! But even if it costs me my life, I'll sit it out here, waiting for it to come up. That horrible curly-haired croupier is deliberately preventing the zero from winning! Here, Alexei, put two of these gold coins on in one go— with one we'll hardly make up our losses, even if it does come up at last."

"But—"

"Go on, put them down. Hurry up. It's not your money!"

So I put down the twenty gulden. The ball flew around the wheel for a while and at last started leaping in and out of the notches. The old lady sat motionless, clutching my arm with her hand. And suddenly—!

"*Zéro!*" the croupier announced.

"You see, I told you so! You see!" she cried, looking at me, radiant and terribly pleased with herself. "Didn't I tell you? It was an inspiration from heaven that prompted me to play two coins at once! So how much am I supposed to get now? Why don't they pay me? Potapych! Where is he? And where's Martha? And where have all the others gone? Potapych!"

"Please, wait a few moments," I whispered to her. "Potapych is standing near the door; they wouldn't let him come any closer. Look, they are paying out your winnings now."

They tossed out onto the zero a heavy roll of gold coins sealed in blue paper, which contained five hundred gulden, plus another two hundred gulden in loose coins. I pulled the lot in with the old lady's money-shovel.

"*Faites le jeu, messieurs, faites le jeu, messieurs! Rien ne va plus!*" the croupier called out, inviting the customers to place their bets and getting ready to spin the wheel.

"Good gracious, we've missed it. We're late. He's about to spin it! Hurry up, put the money down!" the old lady cried agitatedly. "Well, what are you waiting for!" she growled angrily, nudging me.

"But where do you want me to put it?"

"On the zero, of course! Keep to the zero and put as much as possible on it! How much do we have altogether? Seven hundred gulden? So put down two hundred gulden each time. No need to be stingy."

"Come, come, ma'am! There are times when the zero fails to come up for two hundred turns in a row. You'll lose everything you have this way."

"What utter nonsense! Do as I tell you, and stop wagging your tongue—I know what I'm doing." She was actually shaking with excitement.

"The rules do not allow you to place more than a hundred and twenty gulden at a time on the zero, ma'am, so that's what I've staked now."

"They don't allow you to? You're not lying? Monsieur, Monsieur!" she shouted, poking the croupier in the ribs as he sat at her left elbow about to spin his wheel. *"Combien zéro? Cent-vingt? Cent-vingt?* Yes?"

I hurriedly explained her query to him.

"Oui, madame," he confirmed politely. "And then, no single stake may exceed four thousand gulden. That's the rule," he explained.

"All right, there's nothing to be done then. So put down a hundred and twenty."

"Le jeu est fait!" the croupier called out. The wheel spun, number thirty came up, and we lost.

"Go on, go on, play again!" the old lady shouted.

I gave up resisting and, with a shrug, put another hundred and twenty gulden on the zero. The wheel spun for a long time and the Grandmother trembled as she watched it. Did she really imagine that the zero would come up again? I looked at her with curiosity. There was deep conviction in her expression—she seemed to be just waiting for the croupier to announce *"zéro."* The little ball stopped in a notch.

"Zéro," the croupier said.

"See!" the old lady shrieked in incredible triumph, turning toward me.

I too was a gambler, and I became aware of it that very moment: my hands shook, my legs trembled. I felt as if something had struck me on the head. Of course, it was a quite rare occurrence for the zero to come up three times in ten rounds or so, but still, there was nothing that extraordinary about it. Two days before, I had with my own eyes seen the zero come up three times *in a row,* and heard someone who was scrupulously keeping a record of the winning numbers on a sheet of paper say that during the previous twenty-four hours the zero had come up only once.

The old lady, as the big winner, was given her money with special attention and respect. She had four thousand, two hundred gulden coming to her and they paid her two hundred in gold and four thousand in notes.

This time, the Grandmother didn't call Potapych. She had other things to think about. She didn't nudge me either. She had even stopped trembling. She seemed completely absorbed in something—she was all concentration.

"Tell me, Alexei—I am allowed to play four thousand at a time, right? Well, then, put four thousand gulden on the red," she told me.

It was quite useless to try to dissuade her. The wheel spun.

"Rouge!" the croupier announced.

Another four thousand gulden raked in!

"Give me four, and keep four on the red," she directed me.

I left four thousand gulden on the table.

"*Rouge!*" the croupier said.

"That makes twelve thousand! Give them to me. Put the gold in the purse and stow the notes away. Well, that'll do for now. I want to go home. Take me away from here!"

XI

The chair was wheeled away from the table. The old lady was beaming. All our party pressed around, congratulating her. Eccentric as her behavior may have been, her present triumph made up for everything, and the General was no longer afraid that his connection with this strange person would discredit him in the public eye. He congratulated his aunt, affecting the indulgent, familiar smile of an adult amused by a child's whims. But he was really just as impressed as everyone else who had seen it.

Everybody around us was talking and glancing at the Grandmother, and many passed close by to get a better look at her. Mr. Astley was telling something about her to two of his English acquaintances. Some lady spectators looked her over with majestic amazement, as if she were an unbelievable sight. Des Grieux was all smiles and compliments.

"*Quelle victoire!*" he kept repeating.

"*Mais, madame, c'était du feu!*" Mademoiselle Blanche said playfully, with a winning smile.

"Well, yes, without beating around the bush, I just went ahead and made myself twelve thousand gulden. . . . No, what am I talking about? I'm forgetting the gold. Counting that, it should come to almost thirteen thousand. How much does that make in our money? About six thousand rubles—something like that?"

I told her that it was more than seven, and that at the present rate of exchange it might even come to as much as eight.

"Eight thousand rubles? Well, that's nothing to sneeze at, certainly! And I made that sum while you wet chickens just stood around doing nothing! I say, Potapych, Martha! Did you see?"

"Ah, ma'am, how did you do it? Eight thousand rubles!" Martha exclaimed admiringly.

"Here are five gold coins for each of you. Catch!"

Martha and Potapych hurried over to kiss her hands.

"And I want you to give ten gulden to each of my porters—give each of them a ten-gulden piece, Alexei. And what is this lackey bowing for? And the other one too? All right, give them each a piece, too, my boy!"

"*Madame la princesse . . . un pauvre expatrié . . . malheur continuel . . . les princes russes sont si généreux. . . .*" A character dressed in a ragged frock coat and a bright waistcoat buzzed by the old lady's chair with a servile smile.

"Give him a ten-gulden piece. . . . No, give him two. And that'll be all, or we'll never get rid of them. All right, take me out of here. Paulina, I would like to order you a dress tomorrow and a dress for her too—what's her name? . . . that Mademoiselle . . . Mademoiselle Blanche, isn't it? Translate that to her."

"Merci, madame," Blanche said sweetly, curtsying and twisting her mouth into a sarcastic smile addressed to Des Grieux and the General, who was becoming rather embarrassed again and was very relieved when we were out of the Casino on the shady avenue.

"Fedosia will die of surprise when she hears about me," the old lady said, suddenly remembering the children's nurse. "I must give her a dress, too. Alexei, give something to that beggar over there!"

A ragged passer-by with a bent back was staring at us.

"But he may not be a beggar at all."

"Never mind, give him a gulden anyway."

I went over to the man and gave him a gulden. He looked at me quite bewildered and accepted the money in silence. He reeked of wine.

"And what about you, Alexei? Have you ever tried your luck?"

"No, I haven't."

"But I saw a gleam in your eye, my boy."

"Well, I'll try it sometime, ma'am. I certainly will."

"And if you do, play the zero straight away—mark my words. How much money do you have?"

"Just about two hundred gulden."

"That's not much—if you want, I could lend you another five hundred. So take this bundle here. But you, my fine fellow," she said, suddenly addressing the General, "don't go getting your hopes up. You still get nothing!"

The General winced, but did not speak. Des Grieux frowned.

"Que diable, c'est une terrible vieille!" he hissed into the General's ear through clenched teeth.

"Look, there's another beggar, Alexei. Give him a gulden, too!"

This time it was a white-haired old man with a wooden leg, who wore a long-skirted blue frock coat. He looked like a pensioned army man. When I held out the gulden to him, he stepped back and looked at me threateningly.

"*Was ist's, der Teufel!*" he shouted, spicing his remark with a dozen swear words.

"What a fool!" the Grandmother cried, shrugging in disgust. "All right, let's go! I'm hungry. I want to have something to eat right away, then I'll take a little nap, and after that we'll go back there."

"Are you going back to play?" I asked, surprised.

"And what else? Just because you people sit here doing nothing, you expect me to sit here too, and admire you perhaps?"

"*Mais madame,*" Des Grieux said, catching up with us, "*les chances peuvent tourner, une seule mauvaise chance et vous perdrez tout . . . surtout avec votre jeu . . . c'etait terrible!*"

"*Vous perdrez absolument,*" twittered Blanche.

"And why should that worry you people? If I lose, I won't be losing your money, but my own. And where is that Mr. Astley?" she asked me.

"He stayed at the Casino."

"A shame. He's a nice man, that one."

When we got back to the hotel, the Grandmother saw the manager in the lobby, called him over to her, and boasted to him about her winnings. Then she sent for Fedosia, gave her thirty gulden as a present, and ordered the meal to be brought up. While she was eating, Fedosia and Martha kept exclaiming in their admiration for her.

"So I looked at you, ma'am," Martha rattled on, "and I said to Potapych: 'What,' I said to him, 'is our mistress going to do now?' And all that money on the table—I've never seen so much money in all my life—and round the table all those important-looking people sitting. 'Where do all those rich people come from?' I asked Potapych, and I said to myself: 'May the Mother of God help the mistress,' and I got to praying for you and while I'm praying my heart seemed to stop and I'm all atremble. 'May God help her,' I said to myself, and lo and behold, God did help, and to this moment, ma'am, I start trembling when I think of it all."

"I'll rest for a while after lunch, Alexei, and then we'll go back there at around four, all right? And so, for now, good-bye, and don't forget to send me one of those doctors, and I suppose I should drink some of the mineral water here, too. See you don't forget, my boy!"

I left the old lady's suite in a daze. I was trying to imagine what would happen to the General and the others now. I realized that they—and above all, the General—hadn't yet recovered from their first shock. When, instead of a wire announcing her death, the old lady had presented herself in the flesh, thus shattering their hopes of the inheritance, she had wrought such havoc in all their plans that they could only stand there stunned, watching her exploits at the roulette table in a sort of stupor. Now, of course, the fact that she was gambling was perhaps of even greater import to them than her arrival itself. Because, despite the fact that the old lady had twice repeated that she wasn't going to give the General any money, one never knew what was in store and there was still hope. Des Grieux, who was deeply involved in the General's affairs, didn't lose hope. And I am sure that Blanche, who was also rather involved in the General's fortunes (she would be a candidate for a rich inheritance if she married him), even if she had lost all hope, would still have used all her charms on the old lady in an attempt to save the situation, quite unlike the proud, unbending, and impractical Paulina. But now, after the Grandmother had revealed a weakness for roulette and we had been given an inkling of the kind of personality she had (a stubborn, dictatorial old woman, *tombée en enfance*), now, it really looked as if all were lost indeed: why, she was as happy as a little girl at having managed to pull something off, and was sure now to blow every kopek she owned. Good God, I thought (and, may God forgive me, I thought it with wicked laughter in my heart), every ten-gulden piece risked that day by the old lady was weighing painfully on the General's heart, had enraged Des Grieux, and had driven Blanche to exasperation, who felt as if the spoon that should have been feeding her kept slipping past her mouth. And then, it is worth emphasizing that even when, in her first joy of winning, the Grandmother was handing out money right and left, even insisting on taking every passer-by for a beggar, even then she had found it necessary to repeat to the General that *he* wasn't getting a thing. That showed that she had that idea deep within her, and that she had promised herself to stick to it. Yes, things looked very bad now!

All these thoughts were going through my head as I went upstairs from the Grandmother's suite to my little room on the top floor. I was very intrigued by it all, for although I had been able, even before this, to see the main strings controlling the puppets of the show, there were still many points in the plot that remained mysteries to me. Paulina had never really trusted me. And although now and then she had let me into some secret, after she had done so she would always try either to laugh off what she had just said, or deliberately to confuse me, so that finally I wouldn't know what was true and what wasn't. She certainly kept a good deal secret from me!

But now, I felt that this tense and mysterious situation was drawing to a close, that with one more blow everything would be finished, and exposed to the light. I wasn't really worried about how it would all affect me, although I was involved in it, too. I was in a strange state of mind; I had only two hundred gulden in my pocket, was far from home in a foreign country without a job or any means of livelihood, without any hopes or prospects, and I didn't care in the least! If it hadn't been for my feeling for Paulina, I would have abandoned myself completely to the enjoyment of the grotesque spectacle before my eyes, laughing heartily. But Paulina's presence prevented me from taking it like that. I knew that her future was being decided now, although I must confess that it was not her future that concerned me. I wanted to break into her secrets, I was longing for her to come to me and tell me, "Why, I love you, too"; or failing that, if that hope was insane, then . . . Well, what can I wish for? Do I really know what I want? I feel like a lost soul. All I need is to be close to her, basking in her light forever, to the end, until I die. . . . Beyond that, I know nothing! So how could I think of leaving her?

On the landing on the third floor, I had a sudden shock. About twenty paces down the corridor, I saw a door open and Paulina come out of a room. It looked as if she'd been waiting for me to come by, for she beckoned me to her.

"Paulina . . ."

"Sh-sh, keep quiet!"

"I felt as if something had nudged me in the ribs just now," I whispered, "and then I looked up and saw you! It's as if some sort of electricity were emanating from you . . ."

"Take this letter," Paulina said with a worried frown, apparently without having heard what I had said, "and see that Mr. Astley gets it personally. Please hurry. No answer is required. He himself—"

"It's for Mr. Astley?" I interrupted, surprised, but Paulina had already vanished through the door and it had closed behind her.

So they were keeping up a correspondence! Of course, I immediately rushed off to look for Mr. Astley. However, he was neither at his hotel nor at the Casino, where I searched for him in every room. When, angry and almost in despair, I was on my way home, I caught sight of him on horseback in a cavalcade of Englishmen and Englishwomen. I made a sign to him to stop and handed him the letter. We didn't even have time to exchange glances and, as a matter of fact, I suspect that he deliberately spurred on his horse to avoid it.

Was I tormented by jealousy? Whatever it was, I felt completely broken. I didn't even want to know what the subject of their correspondence was. So it turned out that he was in her confidence! He was certainly her friend, I decided (although I didn't know how he had managed to become one so quickly), but was there love between them? Of course not, my common sense whispered to me.

109

But in these cases common sense isn't enough. So now I had one more mystery to clear up. It was getting more and more complicated, the whole unpleasant business!

As soon as I got back to the hotel, the porter and the manager, who rushed out from behind the desk, both informed me that they had been looking for me and that they had been asked three times to locate me. I was, it turned out, urgently requested to present myself at the General's suite.

I was in a truly foul mood when I reached the General's study. He was there in the company of Des Grieux and Blanche. Blanche's mother was not there, and I had become quite convinced that the woman wasn't really her mother at all, but someone who had been asked to act the part to lend Blanche respectability. When it came to serious business, Blanche acted on her own. In fact, it is quite unlikely that the woman knew anything about the affairs of her pretended daughter.

When I got there they were eagerly discussing something, having locked themselves in the study—a thing they'd never done before. As I approached the door, I heard their loud voices: Des Grieux's arrogant and insulting tone, hysterical outbursts from Blanche, and the General's pitiful voice; he was apparently trying to justify himself. When they'd let me in, they made an effort to pull themselves together. Des Grieux smoothed back his hair and his face changed from anger to smiles, the formally polite, French kind of smiles that I cannot bear. The dejected, embarrassed General interrupted himself, but in a strange way, like a machine turned off. Blanche alone made no attempt to change her furious expression, only falling silent and fixing me with an impatient look. I must mention at this point that until then she'd always treated me very off-handedly, hardly bothering to acknowledge my existence, and mostly completely ignoring me.

"Alexei," the General began in a tone of friendly reproach, "I must say that I find it strange, very strange indeed . . . I have in mind the way you have been acting toward me and my family . . . To put it briefly, it is very, very strange—"

"*Eh! Ce n'est pas ça,*" Des Grieux said, interrupting him with scornful irritation; he was decidedly in charge of operations now. "*Mon cher monsieur, notre cher général se trompe*" (I'll translate the rest of his speech, while trying to convey his tone), "he was trying to tell you . . . that is, to warn you, or rather, to ask you most insistently, not to ruin him . . . yes, not to ruin him. I use that word deliberately. . . ."

"But how could I bring it about?"

"How? But since you have taken it upon yourself to be a—how shall I put it?—a guide to that old woman, *cette pauvre, terrible vieille,*" Des Grieux said, getting a bit entangled, "and as she's bound to lose everything . . . Well, you saw her play yourself! Once she starts losing, she'll never leave the table, out of sheer pigheadedness and spite, and she'll go on and on playing and, under such circumstances, no one ever gets even, and then . . . and then . . ."

"And then," the General chimed in, "you'll have caused the ruin of my entire family. My family and I happen to be her heirs—she has no closer relations. . . . Let me tell you frankly: my financial affairs are in a bad state, very much so. You're partly aware of that, I believe. Now, if she loses a substantial sum or, as might happen, everything she has—God forbid!—what will become of us then; above all, of my children?"

At this point the General glanced at Des Grieux.

"What of me?" Here he looked at Blanche, who averted her face in disgust. "Please, Alexei, save us, save us!"

"But what exactly do you expect me to do, General? What influence do you suppose I have?"

"Just stay away from her. Stop acting as her guide."

"Even if I did, she'd easily find someone else," I said. . . .

"*Ce n'est pas ça, ce n'est pas ça, que diable!*" Des Grieux interrupted again. "It's not to stay away from her

111

—that's not what we want you to do. Try to reason with her, bring her to her senses, draw her away from roulette. In short, don't let her lose too much money."

"But how can I do all that? Why don't you try it yourself, Monsieur?"

I tried to sound as naive as possible. Then I intercepted a quick, fiery, questioning look that Blanche directed at Des Grieux, and I saw his expression undergo an instantaneous transformation and become suddenly strangely sincere.

"The trouble is that she won't receive me now," he said with a gesture of despair. "If, for instance . . . later . . ." And he looked meaningfully at Blanche.

"*O, mon cher Monsieur Alexis, soyez si bon,*" Blanche herself said, addressing me with an irresistible smile. She came toward me, seized both my hands, and pressed them. Ah, how that diabolical face could change within one second! At this moment, it wore an imploring expression—such a nice, childlike, smiling, perhaps even flirtatious face. At the end of her sentence, she gave me a discreet little wink, probably to obtain my complete surrender. It was all quite impressive, although a bit on the crude side.

The General leaped up—yes, he actually leaped.

"Alexei, my friend, please forgive me for the way I talked to you when you first came in just now. I said something I didn't mean at all. I implore you, beg, beseech you, I bow to you . . . you're the only one who can save us . . . Mademoiselle de Cominges and I, we both implore you—do you understand? You do understand, don't you?" He kept on begging me, indicating Blanche with his eyes. He looked pitiful.

At that moment there were three polite knocks at the door. It was the hotel attendant. A few steps behind him stood Potapych. They had been sent by the Grandmother. They were to locate and bring me to her without delay.

"Madam is displeased," Potapych warned me.

"But it's only three-thirty."

"Yes, but Madam couldn't go to sleep. She kept tossing in her bed and then she sat up, demanded her wheel chair, and sent for you, sir. Now she's already waiting for you outside the hotel, sir . . ."

"*Quelle mégère!*" Des Grieux exclaimed angrily.

And sure enough, the old lady was waiting for me outside. She was very impatient because it had taken me so long to come. She had been unable to bear the idea of waiting till four.

"All right, let's get going now!" she cried, and we were off to the Casino.

XII

The old lady was in an impatient and irritable mood. Obviously, roulette had taken a firm hold on her, for she paid little attention to other things, and was in general very absent-minded. She didn't inquire about things as she had done before. Catching sight of a costly carriage as it dashed past us, she did point to it and ask whose it was, but I am sure she did not hear my answer. She was mostly sunk deep in thought, emerging only now and then to make fitful gestures and give vent to sudden outbursts of impatience. When we were quite close to the Casino, I saw Baron and Baroness Wurmerhelm at a distance and pointed them out to her. She looked at them blankly and muttered in an indifferent tone, "Ah . . ." Then she turned toward Potapych and Martha, who were walking behind her, and said sharply:

"Where do you two think you are going? Do you imagine I'm going to drag you along every time I go there? Go back home at once!" When the two servants had hurriedly turned around and started back toward the hotel, she said to me, "I don't need anyone except you."

At the Casino they were already waiting for her. They immediately cleared for her the same spot next to the croupier that she'd occupied before. I believe those croupiers, who are always so dignified and try to act like

113

regular public functionaries to whom it makes no difference whatever whether the bank wins or loses, are in reality not impartial at all; certainly they are specially instructed in how to lead players on, and they watch over the interests of the establishment—for which they obviously receive a certain percentage and bonuses. In any case, they looked at the old lady as if she were a sacrificial lamb being led to the altar. Then things happened exactly as the General and the others had feared.

The old lady immediately went for the zero—I was ordered to stake a hundred and twenty gulden each time. We did it once, twice, three times—the zero did not come up.

"Go on, go on, put them down!" The Grandmother kept nudging me impatiently, and I did as she said.

"How many times have we lost now?" she asked after some time, grinding her teeth in her excitement.

"We've already played the zero twelve times, ma'am, and lost fourteen hundred and forty gulden. And, as I said before, it may not come up until evening—"

"Keep still!" she cried, interrupting me. "Play the zero, and stake a thousand gulden on the red too. Here's the note."

The red came up and a thousand gulden were regained. The zero lost again.

"You see!" the old lady whispered. "We've recovered almost all our losses. Play the zero again. We'll play it ten times or so more, and then give up."

But after the zero failed to come up five times, she became discouraged.

"Damn that miserable little zero! Here, put the whole four thousand on the red instead," she commanded.

"Madam," I said imploringly, "that's much too much! What if the red doesn't come up?"

She almost struck me. In fact, I might even say she did, the way she kept nudging, shoving, and pushing me. I had no choice but to comply, and I placed four thousand gulden on the red. The wheel spun. The old lady watched

calmly. She had straightened her back and looked supremely confident of winning.

"*Zéro*," the croupier announced.

At first the Grandmother didn't understand the implication, but when she saw the croupier pulling her four
thousand gulden toward him, along with all the rest that
was on the table, she realized that the zero, which had
failed to come up for such a long time and on which we
had lost almost two thousand gulden, had decided to come
up, as if to spite her, as soon as she had discarded it with
such scorn. She threw up her hands and let out an "Ah!"
that could be heard all over the room. Some people
around us even laughed.

"Ah, good Lord, now the beastly thing has to come
up!" the old lady wailed. "Ah, the nasty, horrid thing! And
it's all your fault, your fault!" she screamed at me, giving
me a push. "It was you who talked me into giving up."

"Madam, what I told you made perfect sense, although,
of course, I can't possibly be responsible for every number
that comes up."

"I'll show you—'responsible for every number . . .'"
she hissed at me threateningly. "Now go away and don't
come near me again!"

"Good-bye, ma'am," I said, and turned to leave.

"Alexei, Alexei, stay here! Where are you off to?
What's come over you all of a sudden? What are you getting so furious about, you fool? All right, take it easy,
stay here with me. . . . Maybe I'm the one who's a fool.
Well, tell me what I'm to do now."

"I can't take it upon myself to advise you, ma'am, only
to be reproached by you afterward. Decide yourself and
tell me what to play, and I'll put down the stakes for you."

"All right, all right. . . . So put four thousand on the
red now. Here, take the wallet. Go on, hurry up, take it
—it contains twenty thousand rubles in cash."

"But, ma'am, that's an enormous sum . . ." I muttered.

"I won't care if I die, if I don't get my money back.
Play it."

I put four thousand on the red and lost.

"Go on, play again, play eight thousand now."

"It's not allowed, ma'am. The maximum is four, remember."

"Then play four!"

This time we won. She immediately cheered up.

"See! See!" she said, nudging me. "Put another four thousand down."

We played and lost; then we played again and lost again, and again.

"Twelve thousand are gone, ma'am," I reminded her.

"I can see that myself," she said in what might be described as a detached frenzy. "I can see that very well, my boy. I can see that." She went on mumbling, staring straight in front of her as though trying to work something out. "Ah, dammit, I don't care whether I live to see tomorrow or not—put down another four thousand. . . ."

"But there's no money left in the wallet, ma'am; there are just some Russian five per cent government bonds and a few bills of exchange, but no money. . . ."

"And what about the purse?"

"Only some small change."

"But there must be some money-changing officers around . . . I was told that I could sell any of our Russian bonds here," the old lady said with determination.

"Oh, there are plenty of money-changers around, but they'll give you such a low rate it would shock a usurer."

"Never mind that. I'll win it all back! Wheel me to one of those shops. Call the stupid porters!"

I wheeled the chair away from the table, then the porters took over and we left the Casino.

"Hurry up, hurry up!" the old lady kept urging. "Lead the way, Alexei, and see that you take the shortest route. . . . How far is it, anyway?"

"It won't take more than a couple of minutes, ma'am."

But as we turned into the shady avenue, we ran into the General, Des Grieux, and Blanche with her mother. Neither Paulina nor Mr. Astley was with them.

"Go on, go on, don't stop!" the Grandmother shouted to me. "I have no time to waste with them."

I was walking behind the chair at that moment, and Des Grieux rushed up to me.

"She's lost everything she won before, plus another twelve thousand gulden," I whispered to him hurriedly. "And now we're going to sell her Russian five per cent bonds."

He stamped his foot and darted off to tell the General, while the old lady's chair rolled on.

"Stop her, stop her!" the General whispered frantically to me.

"Try to stop her yourself, General," I whispered back.

"Auntie," the General said, catching up with the wheel chair, "just one moment, Auntie, one moment . . ." His voice trembled and petered out. "Let's hire a carriage, Auntie, and go for a drive in the countryside. . . . It's unbelievably beautiful . . . from that *pointe*, you know. . . . We were just coming over to invite you to go for a drive."

"Go to your *pointe* yourself!" the old lady said, brushing him off irritably.

"There's a charming village . . . we'll have tea there," the General mumbled desperately.

"Nous boirons du lait sur l'herbe fraîche," Des Grieux put in with a fierce grin.

Drinking milk on the fresh grass is the most idyllic vision a Parisian bourgeois can think of. It is the essence of his conception of *la nature et la vérité*.

"You can take your milk and go to hell with it! Go and lap it up yourself. Me, it gives me a bellyache. Anyway, what are you pestering me for? I told you I had no time to waste, didn't I?"

"Here we are, ma'am!" I announced. "It's right here."

We stopped by the building housing the exchange office. I went in to sell the Russian bonds and the old lady stayed by the entrance in her chair. The General, Des Grieux, and Blanche stood nearby, not knowing what

117

to do. Then the old lady glared at them angrily and they walked off in the direction of the Casino.

The broker offered me such a poor price that I decided to go back and ask the old lady for further instructions.

"It's highway robbery!" she cried, throwing up her hands. "But never mind, change it," she shouted in a determined tone. "No, wait, tell the manager to come and talk to me."

"Perhaps a clerk would do, ma'am?"

"All right, send a clerk. Ah, the bandits!"

When I told him that the customer was an old and paralyzed countess, the clerk agreed to come outside. The Grandmother delivered a long, loud tirade, accusing him of trying to cheat her, and bargaining in a mixture of Russian, French, and German, with me translating the main points. The clerk kept glancing at each of us in turn, gravely shaking his head. Then he looked at the old lady rather fixedly, with a curiosity that, perhaps, exceeded the limits of good manners. Finally his features relaxed and he smiled.

"All right, off with you, man, and I hope my money sticks in your throat! Sell it to him, Alexei. I don't want to waste any more time over it, or I'd go to another money-changer."

"He says you'll get even less elsewhere."

I don't remember exactly how much we got, but it was outrageously little. I came out with somewhere around twelve thousand gulden in gold and notes. I showed the receipt to the Grandmother and wanted to count the money.

"Come on, come on, no need to count it," she cried, waving her hands. "Let's get going, quickly!" And as we approached the Casino, she muttered: "Never again will I play that beastly zero. . . . Or the damned red either!"

This time I tried to convince her to play for the smallest possible stakes, arguing that there would always be time to increase the stakes, once her luck had turned. But she was so impatient that, although she agreed at first, once she'd started playing I could no longer restrain her.

As soon as she won on a stake of ten or twenty gulden, she'd start nudging me and telling me, "Well, you see, we won. If it had been four thousand instead of ten, we'd have won another four thousand gulden, instead of that miserable amount. Ah, it's all your fault!" So I decided to keep quiet, let her do as she pleased, and not force my advice upon her any more, however exasperated I might be watching her play.

Suddenly Des Grieux rushed up to us. The three of them had been standing close by—I'd noticed that Blanche was standing a few steps away with her mother, flirting with the little Russian Prince. The General was obviously out of favor, and she was almost ostracizing him. She hardly looked at him, although he hovered around her, trying as hard as he could to attract her attention. The poor General! He kept going pale and then red by turns. He was shaking, and hardly paid any more attention to the old lady's gambling. Then, when Blanche and the little Prince left the room, he rushed after them.

"Madame, madame," Des Grieux was whispering into the Grandmother's ear in mellifluous tones, "this no good, madame—no win like this," he said, trying to communicate with her in broken Russian.

"All right, why don't *you* show me how to play then?" she said, suddenly turning toward him.

So Des Grieux started jabbering in French, giving her advice. He got excited, explained that she must wait for an opportunity, went into some complicated calculations. The old lady couldn't understand a thing. He constantly pestered me to translate what he was saying, kept pointing to the table, and finally took a pencil and started making calculations on a piece of paper. In the end, the old lady lost patience.

"Enough, enough, go away!" she said to him. "You keep talking such nonsense! You're trying to explain things to me—Madame, it's like this, Madame, it's like that—but in reality you don't know a thing about it yourself."

"*Mais, madame,*" Des Grieux squeaked on, giving her more advice. He was deeply involved in it all by now.

"All right then, play the way he says," the Grandmother told me. "Let's see. Who knows, perhaps it'll work after all."

All Des Grieux was trying to do was to prevent her from risking too large sums at a time—he was suggesting that she play the numbers individually and in sets of twelve. On his advice, I placed ten-gulden pieces on each of the odd numbers in the first set of twelve, and fifty gulden on the set of figures between twelve and eighteen, and another fifty between eighteen and twenty-four. Then, altogether, we were risking one hundred and sixty gulden. The wheel spun.

"*Zéro*," the croupier announced. We lost everything.

"What an idiot!" the Grandmother shouted at Des Grieux. "You nasty little Frenchman, you! Just imagine that monkey trying to give advice! Get out of here, you miserable freak—you know nothing yourself, and you're trying to teach others!"

Des Grieux was terribly offended. He shrugged, gave the old lady a scornful look, and walked off. He felt ashamed himself now for having got involved.

After that, for a whole hour, we tried everything conceivable, but to no avail—we lost every penny we had with us.

"Let's go back home," the old lady ordered.

She didn't say a word until we reached the avenue. It was only as we were drawing close to the hotel that exclamations started bursting out of her:

"Ah, what an old blockhead I am! What a miserable, miserable old idiot!" And as soon as we were in her suite, she cried out: "Tea! I want them to serve me my tea right away, and as soon as I've had it we must be on our way."

"Where are we off to, ma'am?" Martha inquired.

"And what business is that of yours? Know your place, my girl. Start packing right away, Potapych. Pack everything. We're going back to Moscow. I've lost fifteen thousand rubles, you know!"

"Fifteen thousand rubles, ma'am? Ah, dear me, dear me!" Potapych exclaimed emotionally, throwing up his hands, apparently in an effort to please his mistress.

"Stop it, stop it, you fool. Don't start whimpering now and make it worse for me. Just keep quiet and start packing. And hurry up about it too."

"The next train doesn't leave until nine-thirty, ma'am," I said to stop her rushing so much.

"And what time is it now?"

"Seven-thirty."

"Ah, what a nuisance! But what's the difference, after all. . . . You know what, Alexei, since I haven't any money left, here, take these two bonds and change them for me, too, so that I'll have some cash on me on the journey."

I took the bonds and went to change them. When I returned with the money half an hour later, I found all the others in the old lady's suite. When they had learned that she was about to leave for Moscow, they were even more shocked by the news than they had been by her losses. And although her departure would perhaps save her from complete ruin, what would become of the General now? Who would settle his debts to Des Grieux? And, certainly Blanche wasn't going to wait for the Grandmother to die, and would surely go off with the little Prince or, for that matter, with anyone else she might find. And so they stood before the old lady, trying to console her and convince her to stay. Paulina wasn't with them. The Grandmother was screaming angrily at them.

"Leave me alone, you devils! What business is all this of yours? Why must you keep shoving that goatee at me?" she shouted at Des Grieux. "And you, you big heifer, what do you want of me? Why do you keep twisting about before me like that?"

"*Dinde!*" Blanche whispered, rage flaring up in her eyes. But suddenly she burst into loud laughter and walked toward the door. "*Elle vivra cent ans!*" she called to the General as she went through the door.

"So you were waiting for me to die!" the old woman screamed at the General. "Get out of here! Drive them all out of here, Alexei! Whatever I do, you people, it's none of your business. It's my money I've lost, not yours!"

The General shrugged and went out, bowing. Des Grieux followed him.

"Go and get Paulina," the Grandmother ordered Martha.

Five minutes later Martha came back with Paulina, who had been sitting in her room with the children and apparently had decided not to go out at all that day. Her expression was grave, sad, and worried.

"Tell me, Paulina," the old lady asked her, "is it true, as I heard by chance, that that stupid stepfather of yours intends to marry that empty-headed French weather vane? What is she—an actress, or something even worse perhaps? Tell me, is it true?"

"I don't know anything for sure, Granny, but from what Mademoiselle Blanche says herself—and she doesn't feel she has to hide—"

"That'll do! I understand everything now. I always expected something of the sort from him. I've always considered him the most irresponsible man. He thinks he's so important because he's a general—actually he retired as a colonel and was made a general in the reserve—and now he goes strutting around like a turkey. I know very well, my girl, that you people kept sending wire after wire to Moscow asking how long it was going to take the old woman to die. He was in a hurry to inherit some cash, for without it that low woman—what's her name? Cominges something—wouldn't take him as a footman, even if he got himself a new set of teeth. I understand that she herself has quite a neat pile of money that she made by lending it out at interest. Mind you, Paulina, I am not accusing you of anything—it wasn't you who sent those telegrams, and I don't want to keep up old grudges. I know you have an awful disposition, that you're a real wasp, and that if you sting it causes a big swelling. But still, I'm sorry for you because I was very fond of your late mama, Katerina. So if you want, drop everything here and come with me. Why, you have nowhere else to go, and you can't very well stay with him after what's happened. Wait!" The Grandmother stopped Paulina as she was about to answer. "Let me finish first what I have to say. I won't ask anything of you. You know my house in Moscow yourself—it's a real palace, and if you wish you can have a whole floor all to yourself and go for weeks on end without seeing me—if you find me that impossible to get along with. Well, what do you say?"

"Let me ask you something first, Granny—are you really leaving right away?"

"What, did you think I was joking? I said I was going. I've lost fifteen thousand rubles at that stupid roulette of yours today. Five years ago I promised to replace the wooden church in my Moscow suburb with a stone one, and now, instead of keeping my promise, I've lost the money here. So now, my girl, I'm going back and I'll build that church anyway."

"But what about the mineral springs? Didn't you come here to take a cure, in the first place?"

"Why bring the springs up now, Paulina? Don't irritate me, girl—unless you're doing it deliberately. Just answer —are you coming or not?"

"I want to thank you very, very much, Granny, for the shelter you're offering me," Paulina began with emotion. "In a way, you have guessed how I feel about my position now. I appreciate your offer and perhaps I'll take advantage of it, and very soon too. But there are considerations —very important ones too—that prevent me from deciding this minute. If only you could delay your departure for another week or two . . ."

"So I take it your answer is no?"

"My answer is—I can't just now. And, in any case, I can't leave my brother and sister just like that, since . . . since they may really be left out in the cold. . . . Well, if you agreed to take me and the children too, then of course I'd come and live with you. And you may be sure I wouldn't be a discredit to you!" she added enthusiastically. "But I could never come without the children, Granny."

"Well, stop whimpering," the old lady said, although Paulina wasn't whimpering in the least, and I believe never did. "There'll be room for the chicks in my chicken coop, too—it's large enough, thank God! Anyway, it's time they were sent to school. Well, so you're not coming with me now. All right, Paulina, but just watch out. I had your own interests in mind, but I know why you aren't coming. I know everything, my girl. And let me tell you, no good will come to you from that little Frenchman."

Paulina flushed. I shuddered. (So everyone knew except me!)

"All right, all right, don't frown like that. I won't go on. Just watch out that something untoward doesn't happen. You're a smart girl, and I'd be very sorry if it did. But that's enough now. I wish I hadn't seen any of you. Go now. Good-bye."

"I'll see you off to the station, Granny."

"No need. You'd be in my way. Anyhow, I've had enough of the lot of you."

Paulina kissed the Grandmother's hand, but the old lady pulled it away and then kissed the girl on the cheek. As she walked past me, Paulina gave me a quick look and then hurriedly averted her eyes.

"Well, I must say good-bye to you too now, Alexei. I have only an hour left before train time. I am sure you must be quite tired of me by now. Here, have these fifty gold pieces as a present."

"Thank you very much, ma'am, but I really cannot—"

"Come on, come on!" the old lady shouted with such forceful vigor that I had to comply. "And if you're in Moscow one day and don't have a job," she added, "come to see me and I'll recommend you to someone. Well, all right, be off now!"

I went to my room and lay on my bed. I think I lay stretched out on my back with my hands under my head for half an hour or so. The crisis was here and I had plenty to think about. I was going to have it out with Paulina tomorrow, I decided. And what about the Frenchie? So it was true? But what could there possibly be in common between Paulina and Des Grieux? It was really too incredible for words. I suddenly leaped up to go and find Mr. Astley and force him to speak out. He was certain to know more than I did about it. And he himself was quite an enigma too.

There was a knock at my door. It was Potapych.

"Pardon me, sir, my mistress would like you to come down to see her."

"What's happened? Is she ready to go? The train is leaving in twenty minutes."

"She's very worried, sir. She can hardly keep still. 'Quick, quick,' she keeps saying. Please, sir, don't keep her waiting."

I rushed downstairs. They had already carried her out into the corridor. In her hand she held her wallet.

"Walk ahead, Alexei. Let's go."

"Where to, ma'am?"

"I must try to win back my money, if it costs me my life, Alexei. So, off we go, and stop asking questions. Doesn't the play go on until midnight at the Casino?"

I was stunned. I hesitated for a moment, but then I decided.

"Do as you wish, ma'am, but I'm not coming."

"And why is that? What's come over you? Have you eaten something that doesn't agree with you?"

"Do as you wish, ma'am, but I am not coming, because I'd keep reproaching myself for it later if I did. I don't want to have any part of it, neither as a participant nor as a witness. So leave me out of it, ma'am. Here are the five hundred gulden you gave me. I want you to take them back. And now, good-bye!" I put down the roll of money on a small table next to the old lady's wheel chair, bowed to her, and went off.

"What unheard-of nonsense!" the old lady called after me. "All right, you don't need to come. I'm sure I'll find my way there by myself. You, Potapych, you'll come with me tonight. All right, pick up the chair and let's be off!"

I failed to find Mr. Astley anywhere and returned to my room. It was quite late, past one o'clock, I believe, when I found out from Potapych how the Grandmother had ended her day. She had lost every penny of the money I had got for the government bonds that last time

—that is, in Russian currency, another ten thousand rubles. The little Pole, who had attached himself to her before and to whom she had given twenty gulden then, had stayed by her side all the time and directed her play. At first, she had Potapych put down her stakes for her, but soon she drove him away and that was when the Pole came over to her side. It so happened that he understood Russian, and could even speak it a bit, so that, mixing three languages, they somehow managed to communicate with each other. The old lady kept her assistant under a constant barrage of abuse, despite the fact that the man kept assuring her that he "groveled at your ladyship's feet."

"She didn't treat him at all as she did you, sir," Potapych told me. "She at least treated you like a gentleman. . . . But that man . . . I swear I saw it with my own eyes, sir. I saw him stealing some of her coins, just like that, directly from the table. She herself caught him red-handed a couple of times, and abused him something terrible and even pulled his hair, so that everyone around laughed. . . . Yes, sir, she lost every kopek of the money you changed for her. . . . And when we brought my mistress back to the hotel she just asked for a glass of water, crossed herself, and went straight to bed. She must've been tired, the poor dear lady, for the next second she was fast asleep. May God send her happy dreams, sir! Ah, I'm so fed up with being abroad, sir," Potapych concluded. "I warned her that no good would come of it. Ah, I wish we were back home in Moscow already! And what don't we have there? We've a garden and flowers the like of which you'd never see here, at least not with such a fragrance, and our apple trees are full of sap now, and we've plenty of room at home. . . . But no, she had to go abroad!"

XIII

It's almost a month since I last touched these notes that I started taking under the impact of my confused but

powerful impressions. The disaster that I had felt coming
did come, but much more suddenly than I had expected,
and with a hundred times greater violence. It was all very
strange, grotesque, and even fateful—at least, for me. Certain almost miraculous things happened to me; that is, at
least, how I view them to this day, although to someone
else, in the sort of whirl in which I was spinning at the
time, they might have seemed simply a little out of the
ordinary. But the most astonishing thing to me is the way
I myself reacted to those events. I can't understand myself even now. And it has all evaporated like a dream, including my passion, although it was strong and genuine.
But where did it go? As a matter of fact, there are moments when I wonder whether I wasn't insane all that
time, and whether I wasn't sitting locked up in some in-
stitution. Indeed, perhaps I am still sitting in a lunatic
asylum this very minute, and perhaps I imagined all those
things—in fact, am still imagining them. . . .

I've collected all my notes and reread them. (Who
knows, perhaps I did so to make sure that I wasn't locked
up in an asylum when I wrote them.) Now I am all alone.
Autumn is approaching, the leaves are turning yellow. I
am sitting in this gloomy little town (Oh, how gloomy
some small German towns can be!), and instead of planning the next steps I'll take, I am living under the influence of the impressions I have just experienced, under
the impact of the blast of wind that passed by, catching
me up and tossing me into a whirlpool. I keep thinking
that I am still spinning, and that at any moment the storm
in which I was caught will come by again and sweep me
up on its wing, and I will again lose all sense of proportion and direction, and spin, spin, spin. . . .

Later, I hope, I'll somehow manage to settle down and
stop spinning, that is, if I manage to work out in my
mind what happened in the past month. Now I am drawn
once again to my pen and, anyway, I've nothing better to
do in the evenings.

And there's a strange thing—just to keep myself busy,
I go to the miserable local library and read Paul de Kock's

novels (in German translation). I loathe those novels, but I go on reading them just the same. I am surprised at myself. Perhaps I am afraid that a serious book or any serious occupation would dispel the enchantment left by recent events. That may sound as if that horrible dream and the impression it left are so close to my heart that I am afraid to superimpose upon them any new impressions, fearing that they will disappear. Is it really all that dear to me? Yes, of course it is, and perhaps I'll still remember it forty years from now.

And so, I am resuming my writing. Actually, I will be able to tell it all more briefly—my impressions are no longer the same.

To start with, let's finish with the Grandmother. On the next day, she lost everything she owned. It couldn't have ended any differently: once a person with that sort of temperament gets onto the slope, he goes down faster and faster, like a sled on a snowy mountain. The old lady played throughout the day, until eight o'clock in the evening; I wasn't there but I learned what happened second-hand.

Potapych spent the whole day with her in the Casino. That day there was a whole succession of Poles to advise the old lady. She began by sending away the Pole of the night before, the one she had pulled by the hair, and replacing him by another who turned out to be worse, if anything. She drove him away and took back the first one, who was still hanging around her wheel chair, thrusting his head toward her every moment. In the end, she became really desperate. The second Pole she had dismissed wouldn't go away either, and so she wound up with one Pole on her right and another on her left. They kept arguing about the strategy of the play, abusing each other, calling each other foul names in Polish, then making up and jointly throwing the money right and left without any apparent system at all. When they quarreled, each of them staked the Grandmother's money on his own, and it often happened, for instance, that one played the red and the other the black, at the same time. In the end, they completely befuddled the poor old lady so that, almost with tears in her eyes, she asked the old croupier to protect her from the Poles and to send them out of the room. They were immediately ejected, despite their desperate screams of protest; they were both shouting at once that it was the old woman who had cheated them, that she had promised them something, and that now she owed money to both of them. All this was reported to me by poor old Potapych, who told it to me through his sobs, after the Grandmother's final disaster. He assured me he had seen the Poles stuffing money into their pockets all the time, stealing the Grandmother's money quite shamelessly. One of them might beg her to give him fifty gulden for his pains, and then he would put them on the table next to the old lady's stake; if she won, the Pole would claim that it was his number that had come up and not hers. After they had been ejected, Potapych came forward and reported that their pockets were stuffed with money. The Grandmother immediately asked the croupier to take care of the situation, and this time, despite their strident protests, the two Poles were seized by the police, their pockets emptied, and the contents handed to the old lady. Until she had lost everything, the Grandmother commanded the complete respect of the croupiers and of the entire administration of the Casino that day. Gradually her fame spread all over the town. All the visitors at the resort, whatever country they came from and whatever their importance and wealth, flocked to the Casino to have a look at the *comtesse russe tombée en enfance* who had already lost "several millions."

But the Grandmother gained very little by having the two Poles ejected. They were almost immediately replaced by a third Pole. This one spoke perfect Russian, was dressed like a gentleman, although there was something of the waiter about him—he wore a huge mustache and swaggered a great deal. He too "kissed the lady's feet," and "lay at the lady's feet," but he treated the people around him with the utmost aggressiveness and took complete and despotic charge of the game; to put it briefly, he behaved more like the Grandmother's master than her servant. Every moment, before every play, he turned to the old lady and assured her, with the most terrifying oaths imaginable, that he was an honorable Polish gentleman and that he wouldn't accept a single kopek of her money. He repeated his oaths so often that she finally became quite frightened. But inasmuch as, at the beginning, after he had taken over, her luck seemed to be a bit better, she was anxious for him to remain at her side. An hour later the first two Poles, who had been ejected on the Grandmother's complaint, reappeared behind her chair again, offering to perform any services she might think of, even to act as messengers for her. Potapych swore to me that he saw the honorable gentleman winking at them and even slipping something into their hands.

Now, since the Grandmother had missed her lunch and hadn't budged from the spot, the services of one of the Poles could really be used—he was sent to the Casino's restaurant and brought her first a cup of broth and then a cup of tea. In fact, both of them ran errands for her, and toward the end of the day, when there could no longer be any doubt that she was going to lose her last note, there were a full half-dozen Poles standing behind her chair, some of whom had never been seen or heard of before by anyone. And when the Grandmother was losing her very last coins, all these characters stopped listening to her altogether, indeed completely ignored her, reached across her and grabbed the stakes themselves, playing them just as they pleased, arguing among themselves, shouting, exchanging bits of conversation with the honorable Polish gentleman, as if he were one of them; while he himself seemed to have become quite unaware of the old lady's existence. Even at eight o'clock when, absolutely penniless, she was returning to the hotel, four of the Poles still would not leave her alone; they trotted after the wheel chair, shouting at the top of their voices and jabbering away at full speed about having been cheated somehow by the old lady, and demanding that she give them what she owed them. They followed her like that to the very door of the hotel, but there they were ignominiously driven away.

By Potapych's estimate, the old lady had unburdened herself that day of ninety thousand rubles, on top of the money she had lost the day before. One after another, she had changed all the bonds and bills of exchange she had with her. I wondered how she could have borne sitting in her wheel chair all that time, without moving away from the roulette table, but Potapych explained to me that on three different occasions she had had good winning streaks, which had filled her with new hope and kept her from giving up. But then, gamblers know very well that a card player can spend a full twenty-four hours without taking his eyes off the cards.

In the meantime, important events were taking place at our hotel. Before eleven in the morning, the General and Des Grieux had already decided upon some rather drastic steps. Having learned that the Grandmother, instead of boarding the train, was going to the Casino, they went to her in a full delegation (except for Paulina) to have a final and *open* talk with her. The General, who was trembling inwardly at the thought of the dreadful prospects ahead of him, pushed things rather too far: after half an hour of beseeching, begging, and making full confessions, including the acknowledgment of all his debts and even of his passion for Blanche, he suddenly switched to a threatening tone, and even started shouting and stamping his feet; he accused the old lady of dragging their family name in the dirt, of becoming the scandal of the town, and finally told her, "You're a disgrace to Russia, ma'am!" and reminded her: "There are the police to deal with this sort of thing."

In the end, the Grandmother drove him out with a stick (yes, a real stick).

Later that morning, the General had a couple more conferences with Des Grieux to study the question of whether they couldn't really bring the police authorities into it by explaining to them that it was a case of a respectable old lady gone insane and throwing away all the money she possessed—in short, wouldn't it be possible to place her under surveillance for her own protection, or at least to bar her from gambling? Des Grieux merely shrugged and laughed in the face of the General, who had become hopelessly entangled in his own words and was darting about the study like a lunatic.

Finally Des Grieux departed with a gesture of disgust. In the evening we found out that he had left the hotel altogether, after having an important and mysterious talk with Blanche. As to her, she made up her mind that very morning: she completely discarded the General and wouldn't even let him come near her. For instance, when the General met her near the Casino that morning, she was walking arm-in-arm with the little Prince, and neither she nor her mother seemed to recognize him. The Prince also looked away. All that day, Blanche worked hard on the Prince, trying to get him to say the word; but alas, the hopes she had based on that nobleman were quite unjustified. It suddenly turned out that the Prince hadn't a kopek to his name and, in fact, was cultivating Blanche in order to borrow some money from her against a promissory note, so that he could play it at the roulette table. When that came out, Blanche was furious, turned him away, and locked herself in her hotel room.

That morning I went over to see Mr. Astley—or it would be more accurate to say that I spent the morning in a vain attempt to find him. He was neither at home nor at the Casino, nor in the park. And he didn't turn up at his hotel for lunch that day. It was not until after four in the afternoon that I suddenly caught sight of him walking from the railroad station toward the Hotel d'Angleterre. He had been walking very fast and seemed preoccupied, although it was really hard to tell from his expression whether he was worried or simply embarrassed. He shook my hand cordially, as usual, exclaiming "Ah!" He did not stand still, however, but walked on at the same hurried pace. I kept close to him, but somehow he managed to answer me in such a way that I couldn't really ask him about anything I wanted to know. Moreover, I felt reluctant for some reason to ask him about Paulina, and he, for his part, never mentioned her name. I told him about the old lady. He listened attentively with a grave face, but then merely shrugged.

"She'll end up losing everything," I commented.

"She certainly will," he said. "Why, when she went to play yesterday just as I was leaving town, I was certain she'd lose everything. If I have time I'll stop at the Casino and have a look. I'm rather curious."

"So you've been out of town? Where did you go?"

"To Frankfurt."

"On business?"

"That's right."

What could I ask him after that? I was still walking by his side, though. Then he suddenly stopped in front of the Hotel des Quatre Saisons, nodded to me, and vanished through the doorway. On my way home it suddenly occurred to me that even if I had spent two full hours talking to him, I still wouldn't have learned anything, for the simple reason that I really had nothing to ask him. That was it, of course. How could I possibly formulate the question that interested me?

All that day, Paulina was either in the park with the children and their nurse, or at home. She had been avoiding the General for a long time and they weren't speaking to each other—not about anything serious at any rate. I had noticed that some time before. But knowing the state in which the General was that day, I decided an important talk between them on family matters could not possibly be avoided now. When, however, after leaving Mr. Astley, I saw Paulina and the children in the park, her face was perfectly serene. She alone seemed to have been left untouched by the hurricane that had swept over her family. She acknowledged my greeting with a slight nod. I returned to my room quite furious.

Of course, I had been avoiding her and hadn't been alone with her once since the incident with the Wurmerhelms. I had been putting on an offended air, but as time went on I felt genuine indignation coming over me more and more. Even if she didn't care in the least about me, she still didn't have to trample on my feelings in that way and receive my declarations with such contempt. She knew very well that I really loved her, and she herself had allowed me to speak to her about my feelings. True, it had all started rather strangely between us. A couple of months before, I had noticed that she was trying to make me her friend and confidant and, in a way, was already testing me. But somehow it hadn't worked out, and instead we had slipped into our present strange relationship; that's how I had started talking to her in that vein. But then, if my love was so unwelcome, why hadn't she forbidden me outright even to mention it?

No, she hadn't forbidden me. On the contrary, sometimes she deliberately provoked my declarations—though, of course, only to laugh at them. I knew for certain—I had observed it again and again—that, after provoking and then listening to my confessions, she greatly enjoyed stunning me with some demonstration of her utter scorn and lack of interest. And that, when she knew very well that I couldn't live without her! Only three days had passed since the incident with the Baron, and I could no longer stand my separation from her. When I saw her near the Casino just now, my heart started pounding and I turned quite pale. But then, she couldn't do without me either! She needed me. But did she really only need me as a clown?

She has a secret—that's quite obvious. Her talk with the Grandmother gave me a terrible jolt. Why, I had asked her thousands of times to be frank with me, and she knew very well that I'd have given my life for her at any time. But she always brushed me off with scorn, or, instead of accepting the sacrifice of my life, forced me into ridiculous positions such as that time with the Baroness. Isn't that shocking? Is it possible that the only person she cares for in this world is that Frenchman? And what about Mr. Astley? Well, there I definitely didn't understand a thing. But, ah, I was so miserable!

When I got home, I seized a pen and, in a fit of rage, scribbled a note to her:

"I can see quite clearly, Paulina, that things have reached the point where you too are bound to get hurt. I ask you for the last time: Do you need my life? If you can use me for *any purpose*—use me. In the meantime, I'll be waiting in my room—at least, most of the time—and I won't leave town. If you need me, write to me or send for me."

I slipped the note in an envelope and sent it to her by an attendant, asking him to see to it that she got it personally. I didn't expect an answer, but three minutes later the attendant came back and told me that the lady sent me her regards.

At about six in the afternoon, the General sent for me.

He was waiting in his study, dressed as if about to go out. His hat and stick lay on the sofa. As I entered, he was standing in the middle of the room with his feet wide apart and his head lowered, and I thought he was muttering something under his breath. But as soon as he saw me he literally leaped toward me with a stifled cry, so that I involuntarily reeled back. He caught both my hands and drew me over to the sofa, where he sat down himself, then pulled me down into an armchair next to him, and, without letting go of my hands, said in a beseeching tone, his lips quivering and tears glistening on his eyelashes:

"Alexei, my dear fellow, please help me. Save me!"

For a long time I couldn't understand a thing, for he just kept repeating, "Save me, help me, save me. . . ." At last I gathered that he wanted some sort of advice from me, or rather, that, since everyone had now deserted him, he had suddenly remembered me and sent for me just to have someone to listen to him talk, talk, talk.

He was quite out of his mind at that moment, or at any rate, completely confused. He clasped his hands and was about to go down on his knees before me, imploring me, of all things, to go immediately to Mademoiselle Blanche and convince her to come back to him and consent to become his wife.

"But, General," I said, "I don't think Mademoiselle Blanche has noticed my existence as yet. Why do you suppose she would listen to me now?"

But my objections were in vain—he didn't take in what I was saying. Then he spoke about the Grandmother quite incoherently; he was still thinking about calling in the police.

"At home, in Russia," he began, suddenly seething with indignation, "at home, I say, in our civilized country where there are proper authorities—a legal guardian would immediately be appointed for an old crone like her. Well, yes, my dear sir!" he went on, falling into a lecturing tone now, and pacing quickly up and down the room. "I'm sure you didn't know that, my dear sir." He was addressing some imaginary "dear sir" somewhere in the corner of the room. "So let me tell you then . . . for your information, such old women can be kept in order, yes, sir, kept in order, like that . . . Ah, damn it, sir!"

He collapsed on the sofa again, and a minute later, on the verge of bursting into sobs, and painfully catching his breath, he tried to explain to me that if Mademoiselle Blanche wouldn't marry him, it was because the Grandmother had appeared in person instead of the long-awaited telegram announcing her death, and because it seemed almost certain that he wasn't going to inherit a thing from her. He was under the impression that I didn't know anything about their affairs. When I mentioned Des Grieux, he shrugged hopelessly.

"He's left. Everything I possessed was mortgaged to him. I am completely ruined. I don't even own the shirt on my back. The money you brought, you know—I don't know exactly how much of it there is left—perhaps seven hundred francs or so—well, that's all. And what will happen after that, I have no idea. . . ."

"But how will you settle the hotel bill?" I asked, quite horrified. "And then what?"

He glanced at me abstractedly, and obviously didn't understand what I had said, perhaps hadn't even heard it. I tried to ask him about Paulina and the children, but he only muttered rapidly, "yes-yes-yes . . ." and went back to the little Prince, and Blanche's going away with him, and what was he to do when that happened?

"Yes, Alexei, what am I to do then? I swear I don't know what to do! What ingratitude! Well, tell me, isn't it fantastic ingratitude?"

And in the end he burst into tears.

What was to be done with him? I felt it was dangerous to leave him alone, for anything could happen to him in the state he was in. Still, I managed to get free from him by asking his children's nurse to keep an eye on him. I said a few words to the floor attendant too—a very sensible fellow—and he also promised me not to let the General out of his sight.

No sooner had I returned to my room than Potapych arrived and announced that his mistress would like me to come to her suite. It was eight o'clock, and she had just returned from the Casino after her final debacle.

The old lady lay back in her wheel chair, completely exhausted and looking rather ill. Martha handed her a cup of tea, almost forcing her to drink it. The Grandmother's voice and her tone were quite different now.

"Hello, Alexei, my dear friend," she said slowly and solemnly, lowering her head. "Please forgive me for bothering you once more. I only hope you'll be indulgent toward an old woman. I have left over there, my friend, everything I had with me—almost a hundred thousand rubles. You were right to refuse to come with me yesterday. Now I am completely penniless. I don't want to delay my departure another minute, so I'm leaving on the nine-thirty train. I have sent for that English friend of yours —Astley's his name I believe—and I'll ask him to lend me three thousand francs for one week. So please, do your best to prevent his thinking badly of me and refusing me. I am still quite well off, you know! I still own three villages and two houses back in Russia. Besides I even have some money—I didn't take everything to the Casino with me, thank God! I'm telling you all this so that he shouldn't worry about being paid back. . . . Ah, here he is. I can tell a good man when I see one!"

Mr. Astley had hurried over as soon as he had heard that the old lady wanted to see him. Without a second's hesitation and without saying a word, he immediately counted out three thousand francs. The Grandmother wrote out an IOU, signed it, and handed it to him. When the transaction was completed, he bowed and left hurriedly.

"And now, you'd better leave too, Alexei. I have just a little more than an hour till my train and I think I'll lie down for a bit—my bones ache so. Don't be angry with an old fool. From now on, I'll never reproach young people for lack of responsibility, and I even feel I have no right to blame that General of yours either, the way things stand. Still, I won't give him any money, because he's really too stupid for words. But I'm an old fool too, and not much smarter than him. I'm telling you, God will search out vanity and punish it even when it is an old person who is guilty of it. Good-bye then, Alexei. Here, Martha, lift me up!"

But I wanted to see the old lady off. Besides, I was obsessed by a strange feeling—something was about to happen. I couldn't sit still in my room. I kept dashing out into the corridor. In the end, I went out for a walk along the avenue. The note I had sent to Paulina was clear and final, and the present crisis was decidedly final too. In the hotel, I heard that Des Grieux had left. . . . Well, perhaps even if she rejects me as a friend, she still may use me as a servant. She must need someone to run her errands. . . .

When the train was due to leave, I ran to the station and saw the Grandmother off.

"Thank you, my boy, for your disinterested sympathy," she said as we parted, "and tell Paulina that I meant what I said yesterday—I'll be expecting her."

I went back to the hotel. As I was going by the General's suite, I met the nurse and inquired about him.

"Well, I think he's fine, sir," the nurse replied dolefully.

I decided to have a look inside then. But in the doorway of the study I stopped and gaped. The General and Mademoiselle Blanche were there, fairly rolling around with laughter. Veuve de Cominges was there too, sitting on the sofa. The General seemed to be wallowing in happiness. He was muttering all sorts of nonsense and kept bursting into protracted, nervous peals of laughter that drew his face into a network of innumerable wrinkles and made his eyes disappear. Later Blanche herself told me that, after dismissing the little Prince, she had heard of the General's distress and tears, and had decided to drop in on him and cheer him up a bit. But the poor General had no idea that his fate had already been sealed, and that Blanche had started packing and was going to leave on the morning train for Paris.

After spending a few moments in the doorway of the General's study, I decided not to go in, and left unnoticed. When I reached my room, I saw in the light coming through the door that someone was sitting on a chair by the window. The figure did not move when I went in. I rushed forward, looked, and my heart stood still—it was Paulina.

XIV

I let out a cry.

"Well? Well?" she asked in a strange tone.

She was pale and looked dejected.

"Well what? But what are you doing here? In my room!"

"If I come, then it is all of me that comes. That's my way. You'll see. Light the candle."

I lit the candle. She stood up, walked over to the table, and put an unsealed letter down on it.

"Read it," she commanded.

"That's Des Grieux's handwriting!" I cried, picking up the letter. My hands trembled and the lines jumped about before my eyes. I forget the exact words of the letter, but here is what it said—if not word for word, at least thought for thought:

Mademoiselle,

Certain unfortunate circumstances compel me to leave town immediately. You must have noticed, of course, that I have been deliberately avoiding a final explanation with you until the situation cleared up. The arrival of that old lady relative of yours and her absurd behavior put an end to all my hesitations. The poor state of my own affairs prevents me from cherishing any further the blissful hopes in which I indulged for some time. I am sorry about it all, but I hope that you will not find anything in my way of acting that would be unworthy of a gentleman and an honorable man. Having now lost almost all my money in loans to your stepfather, I am compelled to try to save what is left of it. Thus I have already requested my friends in Petersburg to arrange for the sale of the estates he has mortgaged to me. Being aware, however, that your irresponsible stepfather has also spent money that belonged to you, I have decided to forgive him fifty thousand francs of what he owes me and am returning him that much worth of the mortgages, so that you are now in a position to recover all your losses by making a legal claim on his property. I hope, Mademoiselle, that under present circumstances, what I am doing will be useful to you. I also hope that in doing this I am acting as an honest and honorable man.

Please rest assured, Mademoiselle, that the memory of you will remain imprinted on my heart as long as I live.

"Well, it's all quite clear," I said. "And anyway, what else did you expect?" I added angrily.

"I didn't expect anything," she said with outward calm, although I detected a quiver in her voice. "I had made all

my decisions long ago. I could read his thoughts. . . . He
imagined that I'd insist . . ." She interrupted herself and
bit her lip. "I deliberately began to treat him with even
greater contempt. I was waiting to see what would happen. If the telegram announcing the inheritance had arrived, I'd have thrown in his face the money to pay my
idiot of a stepfather's debts, and driven him out of my
sight. I have loathed him for a very long time. He isn't
the same man he used to be before . . . No, no, he is
completely, thoroughly different now! Ah, with what joy
would I have thrown that fifty thousand in his nasty face
and then spat in it, and rubbed it in. . . ."

"But that security for the fifty thousand in question,
does the General have it now? If so, take it from him
and send it back to Des Grieux."

"Oh, that wouldn't be the same thing now."

"Well, I suppose you're right—it wouldn't be the same
thing. And anyway, what can the General do now? And
what about your Grandmother?" I suddenly cried out.

Paulina looked at me with a sort of absent-minded irritation.

"Granny?" she said with annoyance. "I can't go and
live with her. . . . Anyway, I don't intend to apologize to
anyone," she added impatiently.

"So what shall we do?" I said. "Ah, how could you ever
have loved that Des Grieux? What a despicable little man!
If you want me to, I'll challenge him to a duel and kill
him. Where is he now?"

"Just now he's in Frankfurt. He'll be there for another
three days."

"Say the word and I'll take the first train there!" I
declared with stupid enthusiasm.

She laughed.

"Well, he could say, for instance, 'First pay me back
those fifty thousand francs.' And anyway, why should he
fight? What utter nonsense!"

"But then, where will we get the fifty thousand
francs?" I repeated desperately. "We can't just pick up
that much off the floor. Listen, what about Mr. Astley?"

I asked suddenly, as a strange idea suddenly occurred to me.

Her eyes flashed.

"Why, are you yourself suggesting that I should leave you for that Englishman?" she said, looking at me intently with a bitter smile.

It was the first time she'd said anything like that to me, and I believe she suddenly felt dizzy with emotion, for she sat down on the sofa, looking exhausted.

It was just as if lightning had struck me. I couldn't trust my ears. I couldn't rely on my eyes! Did she love me, then? She came to me and not to Mr. Astley! She, a young girl, came alone to my hotel room—therefore she was willing to compromise herself publicly—and here I had been standing before her without understanding! A crazy thought went through my mind.

"Listen, Paulina," I said, "give me one hour, just one hour! Wait for me here. I'll be back! I must do something, I have no choice. You'll understand . . . just be here. Wait for me!"

And I rushed out of the room without answering her surprised, questioning glance. She called something after me, but I did not stop.

Yes, there are times when the wildest idea, the most obviously impossible scheme, becomes so strongly implanted in one's mind that one begins to regard it as something quite realizable. Moreover, if that thought is combined with a powerful and passionate desire, at certain moments it will loom as something fateful, inevitable, predestined, as something that cannot fail to happen. Perhaps this feeling is due to a combination of premonition, enormous strength of will, and intoxication with one's own fantasy, or perhaps something else—I don't know. But that night something wonderful that I'll never forget happened to me. And although what happened can easily be accounted for by simple arithmetic, nevertheless it struck me as a miracle. For how could I have felt so sure about it for such a long time? It is true, I had thought of it not as a chance thing that, among others, might (and therefore also might not) happen, but as a necessity that simply couldn't fail to happen.

It was a quarter past ten when I entered the Casino full of hope, but at the same time in a state of agitation such as I'd never experienced before.

The gaming room was still quite crowded, though less so than it had been in the morning. After ten, only the real, desperate gamblers are to be found at the roulette table; such people come to a resort only for the roulette and hardly notice anything else during the entire season, which they spend gambling from morning until far into the night, and they would certainly go on playing until dawn if it were allowed, for they are always annoyed when the Casino closes at midnight. And when the chief croupier announces a few minutes before midnight, *"Les trois derniers coups, messieurs,"* these people are prepared to stake whatever they have in their pockets on those last three plays and, indeed, that's when many lose all they have.

I walked over to the main table, at which the Grandmother had sat during those past days. It was not very crowded, and I soon managed to find standing room near it. Directly in front of me, the word *Passe* was traced on the green cloth.

Passe is the series of numbers from nineteen through thirty-six; while the set of numbers from one through eighteen is called *manque*. But what did that have to do with me? I wasn't making any calculations. I didn't even hear what number had come up the last time, and I didn't bother to inquire about it before I began to play, as any calculating gambler would have done. I pulled my two hundred gulden out of my pocket and tossed them on the *passe* in front of me.

"Vingt-deux," the croupier announced.

I had won, and I risked everything again.

"Trente et un," the croupier said, and so I won again.

I now had eight hundred gulden altogether. I moved the whole lot to the twelve middle numbers (I might treble the sum that way, but the chances were two to one against me). The wheel spun, and twenty-four came up. I was handed three rolls of five hundred gulden each, and ten gold coins. I now had two thousand gulden altogether.

In a daze, I pushed all that pile onto the red, but then I suddenly came to my senses. And that was the only time that night that cold fear ran down my spine and made my hands and legs tremble. With horror I realized what it would mean to me to lose at that moment—my whole life was at stake.

"*Rouge,*" the croupier called out.

I drew a deep breath. Fiery ants were crawling all over my body. They paid me in big notes. So I now had four thousand eight hundred gulden! (At that point I could still keep count.)

Then, I remember, I played two thousand gulden on the twelve middle numbers and lost; I played my gold and eight hundred gulden, and lost again. I became frantic, seized the remaining two thousand gulden, and threw them on the first twelve numbers—just like that, without any calculation. Well, I must say, I spent a moment of suspense similar, perhaps, to that experienced by Madame Blanchard as she floated down over Paris from her balloon.

"*Quatre,*" the croupier called out. Now I owned six thousand gulden again and felt like a conqueror who is afraid of nothing. I played four thousand gulden on the black. Ten other men hurried to imitate me and play the black too. The croupiers were exchanging glances. All around me I heard suspense-filled voices.

The black came up. Well, after that point, I remember neither what I played nor what I won. I only remember, as in a dream, that I was already something like sixteen thousand gulden ahead, when, in three unlucky turns, I lost twelve thousand of them; then I put my remaining four thousand on *passe* (but at that juncture I felt almost nothing as I did it, and just waited blankly for the wheel to stop)—and I won again. After that I won again, four times in a row. I recall only that I was raking in the money in thousands. And I also recall that the twelve middle numbers came up most often, and I kept with them.

They came up again and again in a sort of regular pattern, three or four times in a row. That extraordinary regularity recurs in streaks sometimes, and it is the thing that can completely befuddle gamblers who keep statistics, pencil in hand. For what frightful tricks fate may play on them with it!

I don't believe I had been at the table for more than half an hour when the croupier informed me that I had won thirty thousand gulden and, since the bank couldn't be responsible for a larger sum than that at one time, they were going to close down the roulette until the next morning. I grabbed all my gold and filled my pockets with it, collected all my notes, and immediately moved to another gaming room, where there was another roulette wheel. All the others at the table that was closing followed me. A place was immediately cleared for me and I resumed my unrestrained, planless gambling. I still don't know what saved me from disaster!

Now and then, however, certain strategic schemes flashed through my brain. I clung to certain numbers and combinations, but soon discarded them and again returned to indiscriminate staking. I must have been very absent-minded that night, because I remember the croupiers correcting me several times. I made the most elementary mistakes. Sweat dripped from my temples and my hands trembled. Of course, there were some Poles who tried to offer me their advice, but I listened to no one. My luck held. Loud voices and laughter rose around me. People were cheering me—"Bravo, bravo!" and some were clapping. I picked up another thirty thousand gulden at that table and they also closed down until the morning.

"Go away, leave now!" a voice whispered in my right ear.

It was some Jew from Frankfurt; he had remained at my elbow all the time, and I believe had occasionally given me some advice on how to play.

"For heaven's sake go home!" another voice whispered into my left ear.

I glanced in that direction and saw a modestly dressed

woman of about thirty, with a face that was pale and sickly but that still bore traces of great beauty. At that moment, I was stuffing the notes into my pockets, crumpling them as I did so, and gathering the gold scattered on the table. When I got to the last roll of five hundred gulden, I managed, quite discreetly, to slip it into the pale lady's brittle fingers, and I remember that she pressed my hand firmly in deep gratitude. All that happened in a matter of seconds.

When I had all my money on me, I went over to the *trente et quarante* table.

Trente et quarante is a game for aristocrats. It isn't like roulette—it's a game of cards. Here, the bank will pay up to a hundred thousand gulden at one time. The limit for a stake, as in roulette, is four thousand. I had no idea of the game and only knew that, here too, one could bet on the black and the red. And so I clung to that sort of betting. The whole Casino was crowded around me. I don't remember whether, during all that time, I'd thought of Paulina even once. I experienced a strange, overwhelming joy as I snatched up the notes that kept accumulating before me.

It looked very much as if fate itself were urging me on to play. This time, as if on purpose, something took place that, by the way, is quite common in the game: it happens sometimes that luck attaches itself to, let's say, the red, and then it will turn up ten, even fifteen times in a row. Only last week, I heard that the red had come up twenty-two consecutive times—a sequence longer than any recorded at roulette; it was related to me as a phenomenon. Of course, after the red has come up ten times in a row, hardly anyone will persist in betting on it. But in such a case no experienced player will switch to the black. An experienced player knows very well what is meant by a "freak of chance"; it would, for instance, seem quite reasonable that after the red has come up sixteen times, the seventeenth time it ought to be the turn of the black to appear. Novices go for that sort of reasoning a lot, and

146

keep doubling and trebling their stakes and end up by losing heavily.

But I, out of sheer perversity, having noticed that the red had just come up seven times in a row, deliberately went on picking it. I am sure that vanity bears at least half the responsibility for it—I wanted to astonish the spectators by taking mad risks. But then—and I remember this very clearly—suddenly forgetting all about my erstwhile vanity, I was seized by an insurmountable desire to take risks. Possibly, when one has passed through so many sensations, he is no longer sated by them, but only exasperated, and then he feels the need for stronger and stronger ones, until he becomes completely exhausted. And I am not lying when I say that if the regulations of the game had allowed me to stake fifty thousand gulden in one go, I'd certainly have done so. Around me, people were shouting that I was mad, that the red had already come up fourteen times in a row. . . .

"*Monsieur a gagné déjà cent mille gulden,*" I heard a voice next to me.

I suddenly came back to my senses. What? I had won a hundred thousand gulden that evening! What would I do with more? I took up the notes, crumpled them and stuffed them into my pockets, snatched the rolls of gold without counting them, and rushed out. Everyone laughed, seeing my bulging pockets and the uneven gait the weight of the gold gave me as I passed through the Casino rooms. The gold I had on me must have weighed well over twenty pounds. Some hands stretched out toward me and I gave it away in handfuls. At the outside door, I was stopped by two Jews.

"You're bold, very bold," they said to me, "but take our advice and leave Roulettenburg tomorrow or you'll lose everything."

I didn't even listen to them. It was so dark outside that I could not see my hand in front of my face. The hotel was almost half a mile away. I had never been afraid of thieves or robbers, not even when I was a small boy, so I didn't think about them now. As a matter of fact, I can't remember what I was thinking about on my way home—I believe I was in a sort of vacuum. I was only aware of a tremendous joy within me—a feeling made up of achievement, triumph, and a realization of power; I am quite unable to describe it. Also, now and then, Paulina's face flashed before my mind's eye. I felt I was moving toward her, that in a matter of minutes I would be next to her, tell her . . . show her . . . But I was not thinking of what she'd told me before I left, and of why I had gone. All the sensations I had experienced only an hour and a half ago now seemed to me something in the distant past, no longer valid, obsolete, something that it was no longer worth remembering, because everything had started afresh now.

I had almost reached the end of the chestnut-bordered avenue when fear came over me. What if I was to be attacked and killed? With each step my fear doubled. I was almost running now. Suddenly I saw the lights of the hotel flashing in the darkness—thank God, I had reached home safely!

I tore all the way upstairs like a madman and flung open my door. Paulina was there. She was sitting on the couch before a lighted candle, with her arms crossed. She looked at me in amazement, and no wonder! I presented a rather strange sight at that moment. I stopped in front of her and started emptying my pockets, flinging the money onto the table.

X V

I remember her looking intently into my face, although she did not get up, or even stir in her seat.

"I've won two hundred thousand francs!" I shouted, throwing the last roll of gold pieces onto the table. The huge pile of notes and the rolls of gold covered the whole table and, unable to take my eyes off all that wealth, I completely forgot about Paulina. I began tidying up the mass of large notes, making a neat pack of them; then I collected the gold into one single big stack; but after a while I gave up sorting the money and started rapidly pacing the room, lost in my private thoughts. . . . Suddenly I rushed back to the table again and started counting the money. Then, as if suddenly remembering something, I hurried over to the door and carefully locked it. Then I stopped in front of my suitcase in profound thought.

"Should I put the money in the suitcase until tomorrow?" I asked, suddenly remembering Paulina and turning toward her. She was still sitting motionless, watching me. She had a strange expression on her face that I didn't like. I'm sure I wouldn't be too far off the mark if I said there was loathing in her expression.

I went over to her.

"Paulina," I said, "here's twenty-five thousand gulden—that's fifty thousand francs, or even more. Take them and throw them in his face tomorrow." As she didn't answer, I said: "If you wish, I'll take them to him in the morning myself. All right?"

To my surprise, she laughed. She continued to laugh for a long time.

I looked at her, hurt and bewildered. That laughter sounded too much like the sarcastic laughter that until recently had greeted my most passionate avowals. At last she stopped, frowned, and looked at me sternly from under knitted brows.

"I don't want your money," she said scornfully.

"Why? What have I done? Why do you say that, Paulina?"

"I don't accept money for nothing."

"I offer it to you as a friend. I offer my life too. . . ."

She gave me a long, penetrating look, as though she were trying to pierce me.

"You're overpaying me, you know. Des Grieux's mistress is hardly worth fifty thousand francs."

"How can you say a thing like that to me, Paulina?" I said bitterly. "I'm not Des Grieux."

"I hate you!" she said, her eyes flashing angrily. "I dislike you even more than I do Des Grieux."

She covered her face with her hands and become hysterical. I rushed to her.

I realized then that something had happened to her while I was away. She seemed quite out of her mind.

"Buy me, buy me! Why, don't you want me? Don't you want to pay fifty thousand francs for me the way Des Grieux did?" she muttered amid a storm of sobs. I put my arm around her, kissed her hands, kissed her feet, went down on my knees before her. But the hysterics did not abate. She put both hands on my shoulders, examining me with great intensity. She listened to me, but obviously did not take in what I was saying. Her face looked remote and preoccupied with something else. I was terribly worried for her—I was under the impression that she was going insane. She would start pulling me toward her and a trusting smile would come into her face, then she would suddenly push me away and again examine me with doleful eyes.

Then, all of a sudden, she flung her arms round my neck.

"But you do love me, don't you? You must love me, since you wanted to fight that Baron for my sake!" She burst out laughing as one does at some funny and touching recollection.

She was crying and laughing at the same time. What was I to do? I was in a delirious state myself. I remember her trying to tell me something, but I couldn't follow her. She was raving and muttering, suddenly bursting into gay laughter that worried me more and more.

"No, no, no, you're good, you're so, so good . . ." she kept repeating, placing her hands on my shoulders and looking into my eyes. "You're my truly faithful one. You love me, and you will go on loving me, won't you?"

I couldn't take my eyes off her. I had never imagined

she could have such transports of tenderness and love. Of course, she was raving, but still . . .

Detecting the passion in my eyes, she'd smile slyly and, for no apparent reason, start talking about Mr. Astley; as a matter of fact, she'd kept mentioning him (especially when she was trying desperately to tell me something a bit earlier), but I couldn't make out what she actually wanted to tell me about him. It seemed to me that she was laughing at him a bit, saying that he was waiting and asking me whether I realized that he was at that moment standing under the window.

"Yes, I'm sure he's down there, under the window. Go on, open it and have a look for yourself."

She'd push me toward the window, but as soon as I made a gesture as if to move, she'd burst into a fit of laughter, so I'd stay by her side and she'd fling her arms passionately around my neck.

"We're leaving tomorrow, aren't we?" she asked with sudden anxiety. "And do you think," she went on dreamily, "that we'll be able to catch up with Granny somewhere along the way? Maybe in Berlin? What will she say when she sees us, do you think? And what about Mr. Astley? I don't think he'll throw himself from the Schlangenberg, do you?" She laughed loudly. "Listen to this," she went on. "Do you know where he's going next summer? He intends to spend it at the North Pole, doing some sort of scientific study there, and he invited me to go along with him. Ha-ha-ha! He says that we Russians can do nothing without the Europeans, and are, in general, quite hopeless. . . . But he is such a kind man, and you know, he tries to justify the General—Blanche is his passion, he says, and that . . . Well, I don't know, I don't know," she said hurriedly, as if she had lost the thread. "Poor people, I'm so sorry for them. . . . And I'm very sorry for Granny too. . . . But listen, how could you kill Des Grieux? You couldn't even kill the Baron," she added with a shrill laugh. "Ah, you were so funny that day with the Baron. . . . I was watching the two of you from the bench; I remember how reluctant you were to go when I sent you. . . . Ah, I laughed so much, so much," she said, still laughing.

And then she kissed me again and embraced me and pressed her face against mine. I was no longer listening or thinking. . . . My head was swimming. . . .

It must have been seven in the morning when I came to. Daylight was glimmering in the room. Paulina, sitting up next to me, was examining the room like someone who has just emerged from total darkness and is gathering her wits. She must have just awaked too. At one point I noticed that her gaze had stopped at the table and she was staring at the money piled on it. My head ached and it felt heavy. I wanted to take Paulina's hand, but she pushed me away and jumped up from the couch. It was a bleak morning, and it must have rained before dawn. She went to the window and opened it, put her elbows on the window sill, and leaned out so that her head and shoulders were outside; she remained in that position for three minutes, ignoring what I was trying to tell her. What was going to happen now, I thought anxiously, how would it all end? Then she moved away from the window, walked over to the table, and, glaring at me with infinite hatred, her lips twitching angrily, said:

"All right then, let me have my fifty thousand francs now."

"Why, Paulina, are we at it again?"

"Have you changed your mind? Ha-ha-ha! Maybe you'd rather keep your money?"

I took the twenty-five thousand gulden that I had counted out the night before and handed them to her.

"So it's mine now, is it?" she asked me maliciously, taking hold of the money.

"It's been yours from the start," I said.

"All right then, catch your fifty thousand francs!"

She flung the money in my face. It struck my cheek painfully and scattered all over the floor as Paulina rushed out of the room.

I realize, of course, that at that moment she wasn't in

full possession of her senses, although I can't understand what caused that temporary aberration. It's true, though, that now, a whole month later, she's still ill. But what was it that put her into that state and, above all, made her act the way she did? Was it offended pride? Was the mortification of coming to me too great? Did my attitude suggest to her that my luck had filled me with vanity and that, just like Des Grieux, I was trying to get rid of her by presenting her with fifty thousand francs? But, in all conscience, I know that wasn't true. I would say that it was partly her own vanity that prevented her from believing me and prompted her to offend me, although she may never have been very clearly aware of it herself. If so, I, of course, was made to suffer in Des Grieux's place and became responsible for something I hadn't done. But then, it all happened while she was delirious, and I knew she was, but I disregarded the fact. Perhaps it is precisely that that she can't forgive me now. Well, that may be how she feels now, but what did she think then? I cannot imagine that she was so ill and delirious that she was completely unaware of what she was doing in coming to me with Des Grieux's letter. She certainly must have known what she was doing.

I quickly stowed all my notes and gold under the bedclothes and left the room ten minutes after Paulina. I thought she must have gone back to their suite, and I decided to go in quietly and ask the nurse how Miss Paulina felt. But to my great surprise, I met the nurse on the stairs. As a matter of fact, she was coming to see me, to ask me if I had seen Paulina. They were looking for her.

"She just left my room ten minutes ago," I said, "ten minutes at the most. . . . Where on earth could she have gone?"

The nurse gave me a reproachful look.

It caused a real scandal in the hotel. The doormen and the manager kept repeating in whispers that the Russian Fräulein had rushed out of the hotel into the rain very early in the morning and had run all the way to the Hotel d'Angleterre. From their glances and hints, I gathered that they already knew that she had spent the night in my room. But there was more gossip going around about the General's suite: everyone knew the General had been wailing and crying the night before loud enough to disturb the whole hotel. People were explaining that the old lady who had been staying at the hotel was the General's mother and that she had come all the way from Russia expressly to forbid her son to marry Mademoiselle de Cominges, threatening to disinherit him if he went through with the marriage; and as he had refused to submit, the old countess had deliberately lost all her money at roulette, to make quite sure that he wouldn't get a single gulden. *"Diese Russen!"* the hotel manager repeated again and again, shaking his head with great disapproval. Some people laughed. The manager was preparing the bill. Everyone knew about my winning by now, and Karl, my floor attendant, was the first to congratulate me. But I didn't care about all that. I dashed over to the Hotel d'Angleterre.

It was still quite early. Mr. Astley, I was told, wasn't seeing anyone. But when he was told it was I, he came into the lobby, fixed me with a heavy, leaden stare, and waited for me to tell him what I wanted of him. I asked about Paulina.

"She's ill," he said, without shifting his heavy gaze from me.

"Then she really is in your suite?"

"She is."

"Well, what do you . . . Do you intend to keep her there?"

"I do."

"But you must realize, Mr. Astley, that it will cause a great scandal. You can't do it. Besides, she's quite ill. You must have noticed that."

"Of course I've noticed it, since I've already told you she is ill. If she hadn't been ill, she would never have spent the night in your room."

"So you know that too?"

"I do. Yesterday, she was coming to meet me and I was to take her to stay with a relative of mine, but she was ill, she became confused, and went to your room instead."

"Is that so? Well, my congratulations, Mr. Astley! And while we're at it, let me ask you something: didn't you spend the night standing outside my window? During the night, Paulina kept insisting that I open the window and see whether you were standing there. It made her laugh madly."

"Oh, really? No, I didn't stand under your window. I waited out in the corridor. I kept walking around."

"She needs medical care, Mr. Astley."

"Yes, I've already called for a doctor, and if she should die I'll hold you responsible for her death."

I was astonished.

"What do you mean by that, Mr. Astley?"

"And is it correct that you won two hundred thousand gulden last night?"

"No, only about one hundred thousand."

"All right. It would be best if you left for Paris today."

"Why should I go to Paris?"

"Why, all Russians go to Paris as soon as they get hold of some money," he said in a tone that suggested he was reading from a book.

"What do you expect me to do in Paris in the summer, Mr. Astley? I love her, and you know it."

"Do you really? Well, I am certain you don't love her. Besides, if you stayed on, you'd be sure to lose all your money, and then you wouldn't be able to go to Paris. Good-bye then. I am absolutely certain you'll leave today."

"Well, good-bye. Although I'm not going to Paris. But please, think of the scandal this will cause. What with the General, and now this happening with Paulina, the whole town will be talking soon."

"Yes, I suppose the whole town will. . . . As to the General, I don't believe it will bother him too much at this point—he has other things to think of. Besides, Miss Paulina is entitled to live wherever she pleases. As to their family—well, one might say quite accurately that, as a family, it no longer exists."

As I walked away from him, I was laughing at the

Englishman's strange assurance that I was going to leave for Paris. He wanted to challenge me to a duel and kill me if Paulina died—what a situation, I thought. I swear I was sorry for Paulina, but from the very moment I had reached the roulette table the night before and had started raking in money, my love for her had receded into the background. I say all this now, but at the time I was not yet clearly aware of it myself. Am I really that much of a gambler? Did I really love Paulina so much? But I still love her, I swear it! And when I was on my way back after seeing Mr. Astley, I was sincerely unhappy and felt guilty about her. But then a very strange, silly thing happened to me.

I was going to the General's suite when a door along the corridor opened and someone called my name. It was the Veuve Cominges, and she had called me because Mademoiselle Blanche had told her to.

I entered their small suite, which consisted of two rooms. I heard Mademoiselle Blanche's voice and laughter from her bedroom. She was still in bed.

"*Ah, c'est lui! Viens donc, bête!* Is it true that you've won a *montagne d'or et d'argent? J'aimerais mieux l'or.*"

"Yes, I won," I said, laughing.

"How much?"

"A hundred thousand gulden or so."

"*Bibi, comme tu es bête!* Come in, I can't hear you from where you are. *Nous ferons bombance, n'est-ce pas?*"

I stepped into her bedroom. She lay under a pink satin quilt with only her strong, magnificent shoulders showing —amazing shoulders such as one sees in dreams, scantily draped in a white lace nightgown that brought out the beautiful bronze color of her skin.

"*Mon fils, as-tu du cœur?*" she cried when she saw me. Then she laughed.

She sounded very cheerful when she laughed, and sometimes she could even be sincerely so.

"*Tout autre—*" I began, taking up her cue from Corneille's *Le Cid.*

"*Alors tu vois,*" she interrupted me airily, "so, start by

looking for my stockings and helping me to put them on, and then, *si tu n'es pas trop bête,* I'll take you to Paris with me. I'm leaving right away, you know."

"Right away?"

"Well, in half an hour."

Indeed, I realized they were all packed. Her suitcases were ready to be taken away. Her breakfast had been served quite a while before.

"*Eh bien,* if you feel like it, you can come with me to Paris. *Dis donc,* how is it you were working as a tutor? You were very stupid when you were a tutor. Where are my stockings? Come, pull them on for me. Hurry!"

She extended a truly gorgeous bronzed leg with a foot that was finely shaped and not at all misshapen, as are so many feet that look so dainty inside a shoe. I laughed and started pulling on the silk stockings, while she sat up on her bed and chatted.

"*Eh bien,* what would you do if I took you along with me? And, you know, I must have fifty thousand francs. You'll give them to me in Frankfurt. We are going to Paris and we'll live there together, and I promise you, you'll see stars in the middle of the day. You'll see women there such as you've never even imagined. Listen. . . ."

"Wait a minute. If I give you fifty thousand francs, what will I have left for myself?"

"Well, that'll leave you with a hundred and fifty thousand francs still, and on top of that I agree to live with you for one month, maybe two, *que sais-je?* And, of course, in those two months we are sure to go through that hundred and fifty thousand francs. You see, I am a nice girl and I warn you of that, *mais tu verras des étoiles,* as I promised you."

"What do you mean? All that money will be gone in two months!"

"Why, does that frighten you? *Ah, vil esclave!* Don't you realize that one month of such a life is better than your whole existence! One month, *et après . . . le déluge!* But I'm certain you can see that! Go on, go on, you're not worth it! But, hey, what are you doing?"

I was putting the other stocking on at that moment, and I hadn't been able to resist kissing her leg. She pulled it away and started kicking my face with her toe. Then she drove me out, calling after me:

"*Eh bien*, my little tutor, *je t'attend si tu veux*; I'm leaving in a quarter of an hour."

When I got back to my room I felt I was already under a sort of spell. Was it my fault that yesterday Paulina had hurled the money in my face, and had chosen Mr. Astley in preference to me? Some of the notes were still strewn on the floor, and I picked them up. At that moment the door opened. It was the hotel manager in person, who until then had never even deigned to look at me. Now he asked me whether I wouldn't like to move to a very nice suite that had just been vacated by Count So-and-so. I hesitated for a moment, and then said:

"Prepare my bill. I'm leaving for Paris in ten minutes."

Why not, I thought—let it be Paris. Apparently it was written in the books that I'd wind up there one day.

A quarter of an hour later, Blanche, the Veuve de Cominges, and I were sitting in a reserved compartment. Blanche was laughing herself into hysterics, and the Veuve de Cominges was echoing her. But I cannot say that I felt all that cheerful. I had completely broken with the past; but then, since the night before, I had become accustomed to staking everything on one card. Perhaps it was true that all that money was too much for me and had set my head spinning. *Peut-être je ne demandais pas mieux.* I felt that, although the setting of my life was being changed, the change was only going to be a temporary one. "In a month or so," I said to myself, "I'll be back here and then, Mr. Astley, we'll see who'll win out in the end!" But I remember that even then I felt extremely sad, although I kept giggling with that imbecile Blanche.

"What's the matter with you? You're so awfully silly!" Blanche cried, interrupting her laughter and turning on me seriously. "Yes, of course we'll spend your two hundred thousand francs, but then *tu seras heureux comme un petit roi*. I myself will tie your necktie for you and introduce you to Hortense. And when we've gone through all our cash, you'll come back here and break the bank again. What did those Jews tell you? I say that the main thing is daring, and you have plenty of that and you'll be carrying money to Paris many times. *Quant à moi, je veux cinquante mille francs de rente,* and then . . ."

"But what about the General?"

"The General? As you know very well, every day at this hour he goes to get me a bouquet, and this time I purposely ordered him to get me the kind of flowers that are hardest to find. By the time the old fellow is back, the bird will have flown. But he'll come flying after us, mark my words. Ha-ha-ha! And I'll be delighted to see him. I could make use of him in Paris. And I'm sure Mr. Astley will take care of his hotel bill . . ."

And that was how I left for Paris.

X V I

What shall I say about Paris? It was all a lot of delirious nonsense, of course. I spent only a little over three weeks there, and that was the end of my hundred thousand francs. I say a hundred thousand, because the other hundred thousand I gave to Blanche in cash—fifty thousand in Frankfurt and fifty thousand three days later in Paris; then I gave her a promissory note for yet another fifty thousand francs, for which, a week later, she demanded cash, arguing that she needed it, since "*les cent francs qui nous restent, tu les mangeras avec moi,* my tutor." She always called me "my tutor."

It is difficult to imagine anything meaner, greedier, and stingier than the type of creature to which Blanche belonged. But that was only true where her own money was concerned. As for my thousands of francs, she had frankly explained to me that she needed them to establish herself in Paris, "to put myself on a decent footing once and for all, so that no one will snub me; at least, I'm doing my best," she added. As a matter of fact, I saw hardly anything of those hundred thousand francs—it was she who kept the money in her purse, while in mine, which she inspected every day, there was never more than a hundred francs at a time; indeed, there was almost always considerably less.

"What do you need money for?" she asked me at times, with the most naive air, and I didn't argue with her.

On the other hand, she decorated and furnished her apartment quite nicely with that very money; and when, later, she took me to her new home, she said, as she was showing me the rooms:

"Here, see what can be done with the scantiest means, if one uses them intelligently and has good taste."

In fact, that niggardly abode cost me exactly fifty thousand francs. With the remaining fifty thousand she got herself a carriage and horses, and also gave two parties at which her friends Hortense, Lisette, and Cleopatra figured, women remarkable in many respects and not at all bad-looking either. At those receptions I was forced to play the idiotic role of host and to entertain nouveau-riche merchants of unspeakable ignorance and shamelessness, and all sorts of army lieutenants, obscure scribblers, small-time newspapermen who arrived in swallowtails of the latest fashion and butter-colored gloves, displaying a pompous vanity such as would have seemed out of place even in Petersburg, which is really saying something. They even tried to make me their laughingstock, but I got drunk on champagne and buried myself in the back room. It all disgusted me to the highest degree.

"He's a former tutor," Blanche explained to them. "He had two hundred thousand francs and didn't know how to spend them without my assistance. And when we get through the money, he'll get himself a job as a tutor again. By the way, don't any of you know of an opening for him? We must do something for him, mustn't we?"

I began to take refuge in champagne more and more frequently, because I often felt very sad and was constantly unbearably bored. I was living with a person of a lower-middle-class, shopkeeper mentality who counted and doled out every sou. Within the first two weeks I realized that Blanche had a natural dislike for me, although I must say she dressed me like a dandy and daily tied my cravat with her own hands. But I knew very well that deep within her she had nothing but scorn for me. I did not care in the least. Bored and gloomy, I escaped more and more often to the Château des Fleurs, where I regularly got drunk and practiced the cancan, which was performed especially indecently there; as a matter of fact, later on I acquired a reputation as quite an expert in that art.

In the end, Blanche came to understand me. At first she had expected that I'd follow her everywhere with a sheet of paper and a pencil and spend my life calculating how much of my money she had spent, how much she had stolen directly from me, and how much there was left for her to steal and spend. And, of course, she was prepared to wage battle with me for every ten francs. She had all the answers prepared for every attack she expected from me. And when she saw that no such attacks were forthcoming, she defended herself anyway. She sometimes started her argument with great heat, then, realizing that I wasn't going to say anything, but would lie on the sofa, staring at the ceiling, in the end she would display some surprise. At first she attributed my attitude to sheer stupidity—I was nothing but a dumb tutor, too stupid to see what was going on; she'd better simply not mention anything at all, so as not to give me ideas. Sometimes she'd go out, and then return in ten minutes or so (that happened during her most extravagant spending, very much above our means—as when she decided to sell her horses and bought another pair for sixteen thousand francs).

"So what do you say, Bibi? You aren't angry with me?" she said, coming close to me.

"No, no, I'm not. But I'm tired of you," I said, brushing her off.

But my attitude struck her as so curious that she immediately sat down beside me.

"I want you to understand that if I decided to pay so much money for them it was only because it was a real opportunity. Anyway, they could be resold any time for twenty thousand."

"That's fine, that's fine. They are beautiful horses, and you'll have a great turnout now; you want it, and that's all there is to it."

"You're really not angry?"

"Why should I be angry? It's very smart of you to acquire things you want to have. They'll all come in handy one day. I realize that you have to keep up appearances, for otherwise you'd never make that million you're after. Those hundred thousand francs of ours are only the beginning, the first drop in the ocean."

That sort of reasoning was something Blanche expected least of all, coming from me (instead of arguments, shouting, and reproaches). She looked at me, completely perplexed.

"Ah, I see . . . That's how you are underneath! *Mais tu as l'esprit pour comprendre. Sais tu, mon garçon,* although you're nothing but a tutor you should have been born a prince! So you really don't mind our money melting so fast?"

"The faster it goes, the better I like it."

"*Mais . . . sais tu . . . mais dis donc,* would you happen to be rich by any chance? No, you're going a bit far, despising money like that. What will you do *après, dis donc?*"

"*Après,* I'll go to Homburg and win another hundred thousand francs."

"*Oui, oui, c'est ça, c'est magnifique!* And I am confident that when you do win, you'll come back here with the money. *Dis donc,* if you go on like this I'll end up by really falling in love with you. *Eh bien,* because you are the way you are, I'll love you while it lasts and I won't be unfaithful to you, not even once. You see, up till now, although I didn't love you, considering you nothing but a tutor—*quelque chose comme un laquais, n'est-ce pas?*—I have nevertheless been faithful to you *parce que je suis une bonne fille.*"

"Now, that's a lie! What about Albert, that swarthy little lieutenant? Why, I saw myself . . ."

"*Oh, oh, mais tu es . . .*"

"Listen, you don't have to lie. You don't really imagine I mind, do you? I don't give a damn, my dear, and anyway, *il faut que jeunesse se passe.* And why should you drive him away, since he was here before me and you happen to love him? Don't give him any money though, do you understand?"

"So you're not angry about that either! You're a real philosopher—*un vrai philosophe!*" she exclaimed enthusiastically. "*Eh bien,* I'll love you, *je t'aimerai*—you'll see, you'll be very pleased!"

And indeed she became rather affectionate toward me after that, seeming almost fond of me during our last ten days. Of course, I never saw stars in the daytime, as she had promised me, but in some respects she really kept her word. And she did introduce me to Hortense, a very remarkable woman in her way, whom we called Thérèse Philosophe in our circle.

But there's no need to go into that. It would make the subject of a special story with a peculiar *couleur locale,* and I don't feel like inserting it in this narrative. The crux of the matter is that every cell in my body was longing for this interlude to come to an end as quickly as possible. But our hundred thousand francs lasted us almost a month, a fact that surprised me immensely. With at least eighty thousand of it, Blanche bought all sorts of things for herself, so that we actually didn't spend more than twenty thousand for our immediate expenses. And still the money lasted that long! Blanche, who toward the end was almost honest with me (or at least there were certain things about which she didn't lie to me), declared that at any rate the debts she had been forced to contract wouldn't fall on me.

"I've never made you sign bills or IOUs, because I didn't want to get you into trouble," she told me. "Any other woman would have caused you to wind up in jail, you know. So you see how much I've loved you and what a decent person I am. I wonder whether you realize how much that damned wedding cost me, just that alone!"

And really the wedding had cost us a pretty penny. It took place toward the end of our month together, and I assume that the last crumbs of my hundred thousand francs went to pay for it. And that was the end of the affair, for after that I was officially put on her retired list.

Here's what happened. After we'd been in Paris for a week the General arrived there, too. He came straight from the station to see Blanche, and from that moment on, for all practical purposes, he moved in on us, although he did have a small apartment somewhere else.

Blanche met him with delighted shrieks and laughter, hugging and kissing him, and it was she who wouldn't let him go. He followed her during her strolls, sat in her carriage when she went out for a drive, accompanied her to the theater, and went along with her when she made her round of visits to her acquaintances. He was still quite useful for that sort of thing—rather tall, with dyed whiskers and mustache (he had served in the heavy cavalry), and a bearing that was still imposing, although he was turning flabby. His manners were excellent, and he wore his swallowtails with perfect ease. In Paris, he started pinning on his decorations. And so Blanche thought it was not only *possible* to be seen with such a gentleman on the boulevard, but even definitely *recommandable*. The kindly, muddle-headed General was very pleased about it all, for he'd never expected such a reception on coming to Paris. Indeed, he was actually trembling when he first presented himself, because he expected Blanche to start abusing him and to have him thrown out; when he saw that his fears were unfounded he was elated, and remained in that state of stupid happiness all the time I was there. Indeed, he was still in the same state when I left them.

I learned later that after Blanche's unannounced departure from Roulettenburg that morning he had had some sort of a stroke. He collapsed and, after that, for a whole week kept muttering like a madman. And he was still under medical care when he dropped everything, got on the train, and came to Paris. It was obvious that the way Blanche received him was the best medicine for him, although the symptoms of his malady lingered on for a long time, despite his elated state. He was quite incapable of reasoning now, or even of participating in serious conversations, from which he tried to escape by answering "Hm . . ." and nodding to whatever was said to him. He laughed often, but it was a nervous, unnatural laughter and it often made him choke; at other times he would sit, gloomy and silent, for hours on end with his bushy eyebrows knitted. There were many things he could not remember at all. He became ridiculously absent-minded, and got into the habit of talking to himself. Blanche was the only one who could bring him to life; and when he morosely withdrew from the world into some corner, it indicated that he hadn't seen Blanche for a long time, or that she had gone somewhere without him, or hadn't said a friendly word to him before leaving. But even then, he himself couldn't have explained what he actually wanted, or why he was feeling so sad and dejected. Then, after sitting motionless for an hour or two (I noticed this twice when Blanche was away, probably with her Albert), the General would suddenly start to look around him, become agitated and appear to be searching his memory for something. Then, failing to remember, he would relapse into his morose immobility and remain like that until Blanche came back, gay, playful, all dressed up, filling the house with her bell-like laughter; she would run up to him, poke him, and even kiss him—that, however, she didn't do very often. Once, the General was so pleased to see her that he burst into tears; I thought that was quite a sight.

From the very first time he appeared in our apartment, Blanche began pleading the General's cause with me. She was positively eloquent on some occasions. She reminded me that she had left the General for my sake, that she'd almost been engaged to him, that because of her he had deserted his family, that I should remember that I used to be in his service and that I should be ashamed of myself. . . . I never said a word, and she kept on piling up her nonsense. Finally, I couldn't keep from laughing, and that settled it—that is, she first thought I was a fool, and later came to the conclusion that I was a very nice and accommodating person. In brief, I had the good fortune to win the worthy lady's sympathy in the end. (Indeed, Blanche was, in her peculiar way, a very kind woman, and I simply hadn't known at first how to appreciate her.)

"You're a nice, clever man," she told me toward the end, "and it's just a terrible shame that you're such . . . such a . . . such a fool that you'll never be able to hold onto money . . . *Un vrai russe, un calmouk*!"

Several times she sent me to take the General out for an airing, as one might send a footman out with a lapdog. Actually, I also took him out to the theater, to the Bal-Mabille, and to restaurants. Blanche gave me money to pay for him, although he still had a bit of his own and relished pulling out his wallet in front of people. Once I almost had to use physical force to prevent him from buying Blanche a seven-hundred-franc brooch he saw in a shop near the Palais Royal. What was a seven-hundred-franc brooch to her? While all the General owned in the world now amounted to perhaps a thousand francs. And, indeed, I could never find out where he got hold of that sum. I suppose Mr. Astley must have given it to him, since it was he who had paid the hotel bill too.

As to what the General thought of me during all that period—I don't believe he ever suspected a thing about my relations with Blanche. And although he vaguely recalled that I had won some money at roulette, I'm sure he assumed that I was a sort of secretary of Blanche's, or perhaps even that she was employing me as a servant. At least, he still spoke to me like a superior to an underling, and once or twice even took me to task for something or other. On one occasion he made us laugh a great deal, both Blanche and me. It was during breakfast. Although he could hardly be described as a sensitive man, he suddenly became offended with me for something, I still do not know what. Probably he wasn't at all clear what it was either. To make a long story short, he started raving incoherently and unrestrainedly, shouting that I was a milksop, that he'd show me, teach me a lesson, and so on, without anyone being able to make any sense out of what he was saying. Blanche laughed madly. In the end, he was whisked away and taken out for a walk.

Gradually I began to notice, though, that he would become sad and seem to be missing someone or something even when Blanche was around. On these occasions he would, of his own accord, try to speak to me, but without ever succeeding in making much sense, although I gathered he was speaking of his past career, his late wife, and his former estate. He was likely to happen on some word or other and keep repeating it a hundred times in the course of the day, terribly pleased with it, although it had no apparent connection with either his thoughts or his feelings. I tried to make him talk about his children, but he'd always start muttering, without really saying anything.

"Yes, yes, the children . . . yes, the children. You're absolutely right. Children are so unhappy nowadays, so un-un-happy!" And then for the rest of the day he'd keep repeating every so often: "Un-happy children, un-happy children . . ."

Once when I mentioned Paulina to him he became quite frantic.

"She's an ungrateful girl!" he shouted. "She's spiteful and ungrateful! She's a disgrace to the family! There should be a law against people like her. I'd have shown her! Yes, sir, I'd have paid her back for everything!"

As to Des Grieux, he wouldn't even pronounce his name.

"That man has caused my ruin, he's robbed me, he's cut my throat! He was my nightmare for two whole years. I couldn't stop dreaming of him—every night. He is, he is . . . Oh, please, never mention him to me again."

I saw very well that there was something in the air between the General and Blanche, but I kept quiet about it. Blanche was the first to talk.

"There's some news," she informed me exactly a week before our separation. "The Grandmother is really very ill, and this time she's certain to die. He got a wire from Mr. Astley telling him that. Now, you must appreciate the fact that the General is still her heir. But even if he weren't, he wouldn't be the least bit in my way. In the first place, he has his army pension, and in the second, he'd live in the back room and be perfectly happy there, while I'd become *Madame la générale,* and that would allow me to enter the best society" (Blanche's constant ambition), "and eventually become a Russian landowner, *j'aurai un château, des moujiks,* and besides, I would still have my million."

"But what if he became jealous and demanded . . . well, you know, all sorts of things like . . ."

"Oh no! He wouldn't dare. And don't worry, I've taken my precautions concerning everything. I have already forced him to sign a few IOUs in Albert's name, so if he ever tried to give us any trouble, he'd immediately get his fingers rapped. Anyway, he'd never try . . ."

"Well, marry him then."

The wedding was celebrated without a great deal of pomp—it was just a quiet family celebration. Only a few intimate friends were invited, including Albert. Hortense, Cleopatra, and the rest were firmly kept away. The bridegroom was very proud of his position—Blanche herself had tied his cravat and pomaded his head, and in his swallowtail coat and white tie he looked extremely respectable.

"Il est pourtant très comme il faut," Blanche told me, as if surprised, as she emerged from his room.

Being only an idle spectator, I didn't take in many of the details of what went on, or if I did, I soon forgot them. I only recall that Blanche's maiden name, instead of being De Cominges, was now Du Placet, and her mother, too, became *la veuve* du Placet. Why they had been De Cominges until then I have no idea. But the

General was very pleased with the change; I believe Du Placet sounded even sweeter to his ears than De Cominges. On the morning of the wedding he kept pacing the drawing room, already fully dressed, and repeating with a great air of importance: "Mademoiselle Blanche du Placet, Blanche du Placet, Blanche du Placet, du Placet, du Placet . . ." and gradually a smug smile appeared on his face. In the church, at the *mairie,* at the wedding breakfast, he looked not only happy and satisfied, but also very proud. In fact, something had happened to both of them, for an air of dignity had appeared about Blanche too.

"I must behave quite differently from now on," she told me with the utmost seriousness, "but then, there's a terrible nuisance I'd never even thought of. Just think—I have to learn my new name by heart—Zagoriansky . . . Zagoziansky . . . *Madame la générale* de Zago—Sago, *ah, ces diables des noms russes.* Well, *Madame la générale a quatrze consonnés! Comme c'est agréable, n'est-ce pas?"*

Finally we said good-bye, and Blanche, silly Blanche, even burst into tears.

"You're a nice fellow," she said, whimpering. "I thought at first that you were stupid *et tu en avais l'air,* but it suits you so well." And as she was pressing my hand for the final parting, she suddenly tore hers away, cried "Wait!" and rushed to her room. A minute later she emerged with a couple of thousand-franc bills. That was something I'd never have thought possible! "Here, these might come in handy," she said. "And although you may be a very learned tutor, you're an unbelievably stupid man. I wouldn't give you more than two thousand even if you begged me, because you'd gamble them anyway. All right then, good-bye, and *nous serons toujours bons amis.* And, of course, if you win again, come to me *et tu seras heureux!"*

I still had about five hundred francs left myself, and also a beautiful watch worth a thousand francs, and diamond cufflinks and a few other items—enough to keep me going for quite some time. And so I am deliberately staying here, in this little town, to organize myself. But my main reason for being here is to wait for Mr. Astley. I know that he's bound to pass through here on business and stay here for one day. From him I hope to find out about everything, and then I'll go directly to Homburg. I won't go to Roulettenburg, not till next year anyway. They say it's bad luck to play twice in a row at the same place. And anyway, Homburg is *the* place to go for play.

XVII

A year and eight months have passed since I last looked at these notes. Now, wanting to take my mind off nagging, rueful thoughts, I have reread them. I stopped at the point where I was about to leave for Homburg. Ah, my God! How comparatively light-hearted I felt when I wrote those last lines. I wasn't merely light-hearted, I was positively cocksure, and full of great expectations. I had no doubts about myself.

But now, a bit more than a year and a half later, I am much worse than a beggar. It's nothing to be a beggar. I wouldn't care if I were one, but I've simply ruined my life. Anyway, why compare myself with a beggar, or with anyone else, and why give myself moral lectures? There's nothing more absurd than dragging morals in at such a time. Ah, self-satisfied windbags love to deliver their lectures with such a smug air. If they realized how well-aware I am of the ignominy of my present state, I'm sure their tongues wouldn't wag to give me moral lessons. What can they possibly tell me that I don't know already? And is that really what matters? The real point is that one single turn of the wheel could change everything, and then I'm sure the sternest moralists would turn to friendly banter and come to congratulate me. Not one of them would turn his back on me. Anyway, they can all go to hell as far as I am concerned! What am I today? Nothing. What may I become tomorrow? Tomorrow, I may rise from the dead and live again! As long as I am around, I still have a chance to be a man!

I really did go to Homburg that time. But then I went back to Roulettenburg, and then to Spa, and I also went to Baden-Baden with Councillor Gintze, an unspeakable scoundrel, with whom I traveled as a valet. Yes, I remained a flunkey for five whole months! I became one when I first got out of the jail in which I had been locked up in Roulettenburg for a debt I contracted there, and from which I was released when some unknown person—perhaps Mr. Astley or Paulina, I don't know—paid the small sum of two hundred gulden for me. So where could I go when they let me out? I went to work for Gintze. He's a lazy young scatterbrain, while I can write and speak three languages. At first I was a sort of secretary and he paid me thirty gulden a month, but I ended up by becoming just his flunkey—he could no longer afford a secretary. He reduced my wages and, since I had nowhere to go, I became his valet. I saved on food and drink while in his service, and I managed to accumulate seventy gulden in five months. So one evening in Baden-Baden I informed him that I intended to leave him, and I went to play roulette. Ah, how my heart pounded that day! No, it was not the money that attracted me so—what I was really thirsting for was to have all the Gintzes, all the hotel managers and the fine ladies in the resort talking about me, repeating my story to each other, surprised at my exploit, praising me, admiring my new victory. . . . These were childish dreams, but . . . But who could tell, perhaps I'd meet Paulina and tell her everything that had happened to me, and she'd see that I'm undiminished by all the stupid jolts of luck. . . . Oh, I didn't care about the money at all! I'm sure I'd have squandered it again with some Blanche or other, that I would have gone to Paris again and driven around for three weeks in my own carriage drawn by a pair of horses worth sixteen thousand francs. By now I should know that I'm more of a squanderer than a stingy man, which doesn't stop my heart from palpitating and pounding when the croupier's voice announces *trente et un, rouge, impair et passe,* or *quatre noir, et manque.* And with what greed do I scan the roulette table on which piles of gold coins, pushed by the croupier's shovel, scatter like glowing embers, and at the yard-high columns of silver stacked near the wheel! Even before I get to the roulette room, when I am still two rooms away, the clinking of the coins drives me almost into convulsions.

Ah, the evening when I took my seventy gulden to the table was a memorable one too! I started playing ten gulden on *passe* again. I'm partial to *passe.* I lost. I had sixty gulden in silver left. I thought it over and decided to take the zero. I staked five gulden at a time on the zero, and when I did so for the third time the zero came up and I almost died of joy—I got one hundred and seventy-five gulden. I hadn't been so happy when I won the hundred thousand gulden. Immediately I played a hundred gulden on the *rouge,* and it was good; I left the two hundred on it and it came up again; I switched the whole four hundred to the *noir* and it was good again; the whole eight hundred on *manque* and that was right. Altogether, I now had seventeen hundred gulden and I had made it in less than five minutes! Yes, at such moments one forgets all past disasters. Why, I've risked more than my life for it, but I've dared and risked it, and now I am once again a man among men!

I took myself a room in a hotel, locked my door, and sat until three in the morning counting my money. When I woke up, I was no longer a flunkey. I decided to take the train for Homburg that very day, for I'd never been a valet there and never spent any time in jail there. Half an hour before the train was due to leave, I went to the Casino to play two rounds—no more—and lost fifteen hundred gulden. Still, I caught my train and came to Homburg, and I've been here for a month already now. . . .

Of course, I live in a state of constant anxiety, playing for the lowest stakes and waiting for something to happen, making various calculations, standing for days on end by the roulette table and *observing* the play, seeing the play even in my dreams—but with all that I have the impression that I have turned into a log sunk in a muddy swamp. I felt like that when I ran into Mr. Astley. We hadn't seen each other since that time, and now we met by chance. I was crossing the public garden, immersed in my calculations—I had only fifty gulden left, I was thinking, but on the other hand, my room was paid for and so I had enough for one more fling at roulette. If I won anything at all I'd be able to go on playing; if I lost I'd have to become a flunkey once more, unless I found some Russian family who wanted a tutor for their children.

Thinking along these lines, I crossed the park, went through the wood, and walked into the neighboring principality, for sometimes I would roam like that for four hours or more and return to Homburg tired and hungry. But this time I suddenly caught sight of Mr. Astley sitting on a bench. He'd seen me first and called out my name. I sat down next to him. At first I was very happy to see him, but when I noticed a certain superior air about him my joy was considerably dampened.

"So you are here," he said. "I thought I'd meet you some day. Don't bother to explain what's happened to you —I know everything about your life during the past twenty months."

"I see you watch your old friends very closely," I said, "and it certainly does you credit that you don't forget them. But wait a minute, that makes me think—was it you who bought me out of the Roulettenburg jail when I was locked up for a debt of two hundred gulden? I don't know who put up the money for me."

"No, no, you've got it wrong—I never bought you out of the Roulettenburg jail, although I knew you were there for a debt of two hundred gulden."

"But you must know who did?"

"No, I can't say I do."

"That's strange. I don't know any Russians around here, and anyway, I doubt that any Russians who happened to be here would bother to buy me out of prison, although back in Russia, Russian orthodox people do buy other Russian orthodox people out of jail. And that's why I thought that in this case, it must have been the work of some Englishman—just doing it out of sheer eccentricity."

Mr. Astley seemed rather surprised to hear me talk like that—he must have expected to find me quite dejected and crushed.

"I must say, I'm happy to see that you've managed to maintain your independence of spirit, and even your good cheer," he said, rather unpleasantly.

"In other words, you're actually quite outraged to find I'm not completely crushed and humiliated," I said, laughing.

He didn't understand me immediately, but when he did, he smiled.

"I like the way you put that, and I recognize the mark of my intelligent, enthusiastic, and at the same time cynical old friend in it. Only a Russian can have in him so many contradictory traits at the same time. You're right, a human being does like to see his best friend in a humiliating postion, and humiliation is the mainstay of friendship— an old truth that every intelligent person knows. But in this case, I'm sincerely delighted that you haven't given way to despair. Tell me, do you intend to give up gambling?"

"To hell with gambling! I'd give it up right away if only . . ."

"If only you could make up your losses? That's what you were going to say, weren't you? I know. And since you spoke without thinking, it is the truth. Tell me, do you do anything besides gambling?"

"Nothing at all."

He began asking me all sorts of questions. I knew nothing. I practically never looked at the newspapers and certainly hadn't opened a book during all that time.

"You've turned into a log of wood," he commented. "You've not only lost contact with reality and lost all interest in world events, in your civic duties, in yourself, in your friends (and you did have friends), you've not only lost all goals in life, except for winning at roulette

—you've even renounced your memories. I remember you at an intense, vivid moment in your life, but I'm certain you've forgotten the best and strongest emotions that you experienced at that time, and your present dreams and aspirations do not go beyond *pair, impair, rouge, noir,* the middle twelve numbers, and all that. I'm sure of it."

"That'll do, Mr. Astley. Please, don't remind me of it!" I cried with annoyance, almost spitefully. "And for your information, I haven't forgotten a thing. I have only temporarily emptied my head of everything, including even my memories, until I've radically improved my situation. Then you'll see, I'll come back from the dead!"

"You'll be here for another ten years or so," Mr. Astley said, "and I'm willing to bet you that I'll remind you of it on this very same bench. Provided, of course, that I'm still alive."

"Enough of that," I cut him short impatiently, "and to show you that I'm not so forgetful of the past, I'll ask you what happened to Paulina? For if it wasn't you who bought me out, it must certainly have been she. I haven't heard anything of her since that last time."

"Oh no, I doubt very much that it was she who put up the money for you. She's in Switzerland now. By the way, I'd very much appreciate it if you'd stop asking me questions about her," he said firmly, sounding slightly annoyed.

"Does that mean that she's hurt you too by now?" I said, unable to suppress a smile.

"Miss Paulina deserves more admiration and respect than any other person I know. But I repeat, I'd appreciate it very much if you'd stop asking me questions about her. You never really knew her, and hearing her name on your lips is offensive to me."

"Is that so! But what else is there for me to talk to you about, except her? Think for yourself—she is the core of our common memories. But you needn't be alarmed—I have no wish to pry into your personal secrets. All I'm asking about is Paulina's external situation, and you could tell me about that in two words."

"All right, but on condition that after those two words

we consider the subject finished, once and for all. Miss Paulina was ill for a long time; in fact, she is still ill. . . . For some time she stayed with my mother and sister in northern England. About six months ago, her Grandmother—that eccentric old lady, remember?—died and left her seven thousand pounds in her will. Now Miss Paulina is traveling with my sister. Miss Paulina's young brother and sister were also taken care of in the old lady's will and are now going to school in London. The General, Miss Paulina's stepfather, died of a stroke last month in Paris. Mademoiselle Blanche was treating him quite well, although she managed to transfer to her own bank account everything he got from his old aunt. Well, I believe that covers everything."

"And what about Des Grieux? Is he traveling in Switzerland now too?"

"No, he's not traveling in Switzerland and I don't know where he is. Besides, let me warn you once and for all that you'd better avoid such ungentlemanly insinuations and association of names; otherwise you'll have to answer to me for it."

"What do you mean? You'd disregard our old friendship?"

"Yes, I'd disregard our old friendship."

"Well, Mr. Astley, if that's so, please accept my apologies. But still, I don't see anything ungentlemanly in what I said—I never accused Miss Paulina of anything. Besides, neither you nor I can possibly understand anything about such things as associations between Frenchmen and Russian girls. It is quite beyond us."

"If you would stop coupling Des Grieux's name with that other name, I'd be very curious to know what you mean by 'associations between Frenchmen and Russian girls'. Why precisely a Russian girl and a Frenchman?"

"You see, I've managed to get you interested. It is a long story, Mr. Astley, and a very important matter, although at first it may sound rather ridiculous. A Frenchman, Mr. Astley, is a beautiful, finished product in an established, formal tradition. You, being British, may not approve of such perfection of form; I, being a Russian, do not approve of it either, although that may be out of sheer envy, but then, our young ladies may be of a quite different opinion. By the same token, you may find their Racine affected, contrived, and perfumed, even ridiculous in a way, and probably you couldn't even bear to read his stuff. Now I find him all that too, but he has a lot of charm, and whatever we may say, he *is* a great poet. The French traditional form had begun to acquire elegance at a time when we were still wild bears. Then the Revolution took over from the aristocracy, and now the most miserable little Frenchie has nice manners, knows how to express himself, and even thinks in elegant forms, without having to engage either his brain or his heart in his way of thinking and expressing himself—all that he has acquired by inheritance; while underneath he may be the most empty-headed creature and thoroughly vulgar at heart. And now, Mr. Astley, let me tell you that there is no more trusting creature in the world than an intelligent, kind-hearted, and not over-sophisticated Russian girl. A Des Grieux, appearing in any guise, in any role, can conquer her heart with incredible ease—he possesses that graceful form, Mr. Astley, and the young girl accepts that form as his personal character, his personal style, instead of seeing in it an external garment that he has inherited. Although it may sound unpleasant to your ears, I must tell you that your fellow countrymen are for the most part awkward and charmless—we Russians are quite adept at detecting charm and are very sensitive to it. But spiritual beauty and individual originality require much more independence of judgment and certainly more experience to detect than our women, especially our young ladies, can muster. Now, it would take Miss Paulina—oh, please forgive that slip; I wish I could take it back—a long time to make up her mind to chose you over that nasty creature Des Grieux. Ah, I know, she'll appreciate you and open her heart to you, but then that nasty, petty crook and usurer Des Grieux will still rule over it. Yes, and she will keep him there out of sheer stubbornness, out of a sort of vanity, just because Des Grieux once appeared to her with the halo of a refined marquis, a blasé liberal who had ostensibly squandered his fortune trying to help her family and the irresponsible General. And although all his tricks may be exposed later, that doesn't make the slightest difference—she still longs for Des Grieux as he appeared to her in the first place; he's the one she needs. And the more she comes to hate the actual Des Grieux, the more she pines for the other one, although he only existed in her imagination. Are you in the sugar business, Mr. Astley?"

"Yes, I'm a partner in the sugar refinery of Lovell & Co."

"So you see, Mr. Astley, her choice is between a man in the sugar business and that Apollo Belvedere. Well, they don't go together very well. As to me, I'm not even a sugar man, but just a common, small-time roulette player who has even been a flunkey, a fact of which I'm sure Miss Paulina is already aware, since, I understand, she has a well-informed spying agency."

"You're bitter, and that's why you're talking all this nonsense," Mr. Astley said coldly after a brief pause. "Besides, there's nothing so very original in your words."

"You're right there! But then, that makes it all the worse, my honorable friend, because however hackneyed all these accusations may be, however overworked and melodramatic they may sound, they are nonetheless absolutely true. And whatever you may say, neither of us has got anywhere."

"What disgusting rot! And so . . . and so . . ." Mr. Astley said, his eyes glaring, "and so, let me tell you, you ungrateful, unworthy, petty, unhappy man, that I came to Homburg at her special request, because she wanted me to see you, to have a long, friendly talk with you and then report to her everything about you—your thoughts, your feelings, your hopes, and . . . and your memories."

"Really, reallly?" I cried, and the tears poured from my eyes. I could not hold them back. I believe it was the first time in my life I had wept like that.

"Yes, you unfortunate man, she did love you. I can tell

you so because, anyway, you're a lost man. And even if I told you that she was in love with you to this day, you'd still remain here, wouldn't you? Yes, you've ruined your life. You were once a quite able and lively person, a rather good man, on the whole; you could even have been a useful citizen of your country, which so badly needs such people. But now, you'll stay here till the end. I'm not blaming you, and I feel that most Russians are like you or could easily become so. And if it weren't roulette, it would be one of many other similar things. The exceptions among them are all too rare. You're not the first Russian to be unable to understand what hard work means, and of course I'm not speaking of your common people. Roulette is mostly a Russian game. So far, you've been honest and have preferred becoming a flunkey to stealing, but I hate to think what might happen in the future. Well, enough of this. Good-bye now. I'm sure you need money, so here are ten louis d'or for you—I won't give you any more because you'll lose it anyway. Take it, and good-bye. Well, go on, take it, then!"

"No, Mr. Astley, after all that has just been said—"

"Take it!" he shouted. "I know you're still a gentleman and I'm giving it to you as a friend gives to his true friend. If I could be certain that you would immediately give up gambling and leave Homburg for Russia, I'd be prepared to let you have a thousand pounds right away, to start you off on a new career. And if I am giving you only ten louis d'or instead of the thousand pounds it is precisely because, as things stand, the amount can't make the slightest difference—whatever it is, you'll lose it. So take it, and good-bye."

"All right, I'll take it, if you'll let me embrace you at parting."

"Ah, that, of course, with pleasure."

We embraced with sincere feeling and Mr. Astley walked off.

No, he isn't right. If I had said rude and stupid things about Paulina and Des Grieux, he had made superficial and unwarranted remarks about the Russians. I don't object to what he said about me personally. But after all ... well, it's nothing but words, words, words, and what we need is action, not words. The main thing is Switzerland, of course. Ah, if I could go there tomorrow! I could recover there, come back to life. I ought to prove it to them. . . . Let Paulina see that I can still become a man. It will only take me . . . It's too late today, but tomorrow ... Ah, I have a premonition—I can't miss! I have fifteen louis d'or now, instead of the ten gulden I was going to start playing with. If I start very carefully . . . Why am I really such an irresponsible infant? Can't I see that I am a doomed man? But why can't I come back to life? All I have to do is to be calculating and patient once, and I'll make it! I have to hold out for just one hour, and then my whole life will be different. The main thing is a strong will. Just remember what happened to me seven months ago in Roulettenburg, before I lost everything. Oh, it was a beautiful instance of determination. . . . I lost everything I had then. . . . I walked out of the Casino, and suddenly discovered that I still had one gulden in my waistcoat pocket. Well, that'll pay for my dinner at least, I said to myself. But after I had taken a hundred steps or so, I changed my mind and went back to the roulette table. I staked that gulden on *manque* (yes, that time I played *manque*). And it's true, it gives you a special feeling when you are all alone in a foreign country, far away from your home and your friends, not knowing whether you're going to eat that day, and gambling your very last gulden! I won, and twenty minutes later I left the Casino with one hundred and seventy gulden in my pocket. It's the absolute truth! That's what your very last gulden can sometimes do for you! But suppose I had lost heart then? What if I hadn't dared to risk? . . .

Tomorrow, tomorrow, it will all be over!

THE END